Negro Island Light

Negro Island Light

Claudette Lewis Bard

Negro Island Light

Copyright © 2016 by Claudette Lewis Bard

Cover Design by: Ed Bard

Book Website: cvlb.wixsite.com/cvlb
Email: cvlbard@comcast.net

Give feedback on the book at:
cvlbard@comcast.net
Printed in U.S.A

Dedicated to my loving husband, Ed.

Thank you for your endless encouragement, limitless knowledge of the technical aspects, persistence in showing me a different viewpoint and your never-ending faith in me that I often did not have.
Love you, CLB.

Acknowledgments

To my Dad, whose personality and characteristics are sporadically mirrored in this work. He gave me lessons too numerous to mention and I take them with me daily.

To Mom, who always had faith in whatever I chose to do. Her love for reading the written word brought me to this point. Thank you for introducing me to the music of Erroll Gardner and other classic African American artists of the 1940s and 50s; it gave me inspiration for this work.

To Mr. Sussman who taught my Pegasus class, a remedial English 101 course at Montgomery College in Rockville, Md. He taught me that writing is not just a listing of events and then coming up with an ending. It is telling a story. The story should come from deep within your soul and your heart. So reach down, dig deep, find the words and bring it forward.

To my brothers and sisters whose many traits, characteristics, habits, and personalities are, at some point, reflected in this work.

And lastly, to my loving husband who pushes me beyond my boundaries to places that I need to go but don't often want to. He makes sure I get there even though he faces constant resistance. Thank you, Ed, for putting up with the battles.

Prologue

Dear Diary,
Tuesday, July 27, 1982

We're here in Maine—again—and I have yet to understand why Daddy likes this place. There isn't a thing to do. Yeah, we're officially in Maine and I know this because we crossed the Piscataqua River Bridge earlier this afternoon. I tried to write earlier but Daddy seemed to hit every pot hole in the road. But we finally made it to Camden and thank goodness I'm out of that car. But I must admit, the scenery is not bad, for sure.

I'm in my room now, my home away from home. That was one long drive from Maryland. When Daddy and I arrived, Mr. Henry and Miss Martha from next door greeted us with open arms and Mr. Henry snapped a picture. I mean, how corny is that? Geez. We stood in front of our cottage that Daddy said he and Mommy bought even before I was born and Mr. Henry snapped away. I so want to be back with my friends in Silver Spring, going to the mall and looking at boys or buying the latest albums or cassette or another pair of earrings. I miss my friends so much when we come here. Maybe next year Julia can come with us and it can be somewhat bearable. She's my best friend and she's an absolute blast to be around. We would have so much fun laughing at this drab town. Well, let me put this cassette in the player and blast some Earth, Wind & Fire or maybe some Toto. I'm sure Daddy will bang on my door, telling me to turn down my music. He just doesn't appreciate good rock and roll; he likes that old timey stuff, Nat "King" Cole, Ella Fitzgerald and somebody named Erroll Garner. Hopefully some TV station has music videos to watch. Until I write tomorrow…

Chapter 1

Laid Off

Eugenia never imagined this day would come after 21 years at the same company. Well, she had a hint at some point. Yes, there were rumors of a takeover, a buyout. Then the takeover happened, but upper management assured the employees that no one was losing their job. But it was in the cards—after all, the other bank already had a marketing department. Why would they need the "dinosaurs", the knowledgeable, experienced workers from her bank? They had their own people, much younger and cheaper, too. One by one, Eugenia saw co-workers go and then the inevitable—the package— the walking papers were offered to her. Her choices were to take the package or a part-time position. Eugenia decided that it was time to go—she couldn't afford to work part-time. And besides, why stay at a company that doesn't want you?

Silently Eugenia packed her box of belongings—*how did I accumulate so much stuff,* she thought. *Oh yeah, 21 years.* She collected her plants, little knickknacks, some certificates for outstanding service to customers, a picture of her and her father with the cottage in the background.

She then stopped and stared at the picture. *Why does this always happen? —I always have to stop and look at the pictures.* Yeah, she must have been 12 or so. A neighbor snapped the picture of the two of them standing in front of the cottage that was their summer home, Eugenia's father with his arm around her shoulder. Each with a grin on their faces so wide, anyone seeing them had no doubt that they were happy. Father and daughter, although most said that she didn't resemble him at all—Eugenia with her fair African American complexion and her father's mahogany hue. Those who knew her mother said Eugenia's resemblance to her mother was uncanny.

Eugenia stuffed the picture carefully in the box on top of everything else and paused for a moment. Researchers say that losing one's job is like a death in the family. If that's true, Eugenia has suffered two deaths in the past six months—first losing her dad six months ago and now this, the layoff. She collected her thoughts and proceeded to finish her task. Bernard, one of the guys from the mailroom, appeared with a cart and helped load the boxes to take them down to her car out front of the office building. As the elevator descended, Bernard told her how much she would be missed and made small talk. They placed all the boxes in the car and Eugenia went one more time up in the elevator, said her good-byes, exchanged hugs and left the building for the last time

She got into her car and drove away. At last, she found a shopping center parking lot, went to a secluded area where only a few cars were parked, turned off her engine and burst into tears, hoping no one would see her.

The displacement package consisted of six months of working with a job placement service, including resume writing, job hunting techniques, and various ways to get back into the work force. She was entitled to six months of severance pay that included medical and options to continue her education. All in all, it sounded pretty good. But how does one deal with the loss, the loss that included no job to go to each day, no co-workers, although she could contact former co-workers in the same boat. There were quite a few. How does one deal with the uncertainty of "what if I am not working in six months"? Is that answer in the package?

After a few minutes, Eugenia wiped away her tears and blew her nose, pulled herself together and got back on the road for home. While stopped at a traffic light she saw a destitute woman, thin from, no doubt, lack of food, dirty hair and skin weathered by the sun. The down-and-out woman walked slowly back and forth on the median, carrying a sign that read 'Homeless. Please Help. God bless you' and holding a cup to collect any money drivers were willing to give. For one fleeting moment, Eugenia envisioned that that could be her. Opening her window, she handed the woman a couple of dollars. The woman graciously thanked her and Eugenia drove on home.

After carrying the boxes up the three flights of steps to her condo, Eugenia decided that she would start her job search tomorrow, look into attending the workshops and sessions offered by the placement service and assess her financial situation. Today was a day to sit in front of the TV, pick a free movie on demand or watch movies on the Lifetime Network, eat peanut butter on Ritz, tackle some ice cream and veg out.

Chapter 2

Let's Get Started

The one good thing about not having a job is that Eugenia had the time to exercise each morning, a goal that she has had for a long time. She hit the quarter mile track at the local high school, put her earplugs in, got into a good walking pace and set out to continue her life—her new life and another chapter. *I had planned on going to the cottage next week*, she thought. She had planned a vacation for next week. *Well, I guess I don't have to wait since I ain't fucking working*, she thought.

But she decided to go when she had planned to—next week—tying up loose ends here, getting her resume together and leaving when planned. It would be so nice to get out of the D.C. area, away from the traffic and humidity that seem to plague the summers, especially these July days. Maine should be more pleasant.

It was Wednesday and Eugenia was planning to leave next Monday. She needed to look into her packet from the exit interview, go online for information about the placement service, make plans to attend some workshops and continue to look for work.

After her walk, Eugenia spent most of the morning online, putting her resume on several career websites, updating her LinkedIn profile, looking for jobs and then, in the afternoon, unpacking her box from work. She found the picture of her and her father in front of the cottage and began thinking about the times that they had.

Charles Watts was a tall man, brown-skinned with a smile that seemed to light up his entire face and a laugh to go with it. After Eugenia's mother died of breast cancer when Eugenia was around three, Chuck, as he always insisted people call him, devoted his life to raising his only daughter. And he had five sisters to help. Chuck was the youngest child and only boy so after his wife died, his sisters, especially his sister Nell, did not hesitate to help her younger brother. Nell, who was 15 months older than he and lived nearby, had never married and was a nurse at an area hospital. She stepped up to the plate and has always thought of Eugenia as her own daughter.

Nell taught him how to plait hair, buy girl's clothing and even told him how to explain to his daughter about menstruation and the facts of life, although she was there to help, as Chuck fumbled through the explanation. Chuck showed Eugenia the parts of a car after she bought her first one at age 18, teaching her how to change a tire and change the oil. They attended Orioles' games whenever they could travel out of the D.C. area to Baltimore since Chuck's beloved Senators had left D.C. years ago and the city had not yet put a new team in place. And Chuck loved the Washington Redskins and often would take Eugenia to a game when he could get tickets.

Aunt Nell made sure Eugenia knew how to be a lady, balancing out all of the male perspective influence that Chuck put on his daughter. The hardest part for Chuck, needless to say, was the teenage years when Eugenia started dating. He made sure that the boys came by the house, picked her up and abided by the curfew. Aunt Nell was there to help as well and made sure Chuck didn't bring out his shotgun. And, yes, he had one.

Eugenia set the picture on a shelf in her living room. Sitting down in her comfortable chair, she began to cry again. It is often said that God doesn't put more on you than you can handle—Eugenia was wondering whether this was a test of her endurance. It all seemed more than she could tolerate.

On Thursday and Friday, Eugenia attended some workshops and worked one-on-one with a professional resume writer who helped her put together a resume. The placement center also offered usage of their computers and a "Job Club" where displaced workers could get counseling and talk to other job seekers about their job loss. Eugenia was feeling a little better about her situation and the services offered were extremely helpful.

She ran into other displaced co-workers and they all went out to dinner Friday night. Some had been out of work longer than she had and they offered tips on dealing with the job loss. They also bitched and told stories about the approach upper management took in dealing with the layoffs. Eugenia thought she was on the way to getting through this chapter of her life and felt that she was on better footing.

Saturday came and she knew that she had to start packing since she was leaving Monday morning for her stay in the cottage in Camden, Maine. She was driving up and anticipated a 9 to 10-hour drive. Eugenia had planned to be away for two weeks and made sure all her bills were paid.

Eugenia saw that all her affairs were in order. Sophia, her neighbor and trusted friend, would watch her condo. Sophia was divorced and lived across the hall. She was in her 60s, Italian, retired and had a crass personality, to say the least. She told you how she felt and didn't mince words. They got along fine and when one of them went out of town, they watched each other's place. And even though it was date night, neither one of them had a date. Eugenia broke up with her last boyfriend about a year ago. She had dated sporadically but nothing seemed to take. Her last boyfriend seemed to want two women and Eugenia refused to accept those terms. *I'm too old for that shit,* she thought.

So the two women sat out on Eugenia's balcony that evening, shared a bottle of Moscato, and assessed Eugenia's trip to New England.

"When was the last time you were there, Eugenia?" asked Sophia.

"Oh my God, I guess I must have been 14, maybe 15. It's been a while. My dad kept begging me to come every year, but you know when you're a teenager, you want to hang with your friends. Then I started working at 16, especially during the summers and that's usually when he went. I wanted to earn that money."

"Fourteen or fifteen? Christ, what are you 45 now?" asked Sophia.

"Yeah," as she took a sip of her wine. "Of course, I wish I had gone…now." She looked over at Sophia, barely seeing her face in the fading evening light. The sun had set by now and Eugenia didn't feel like getting up to turn on a light inside her condo. "I miss him, Sophia." Sophia reached over and squeezed her hand.

"I know, dear." They sat in silence for a few more minutes.

Sophia felt the tension in the air and broke the silence. "Hey, do you think there're any single, cute older men in that one-horse town?"

Eugenia looked over at her and smiled. "I don't know. But if there are, I'll let you know and you can come up and check them out."

"Sounds like a plan. Here's to new beginnings!" Sophia raised her glass, tapped it against Eugenia's and continued the toast. "You're embarking on a new chapter in your life, girl. I know, it doesn't seem like it but you know what they say, 'when one door closes, another door opens'. I know that sounds corny; I know it's a cliché."

She then leaned forward and could see the sad look on Eugenia's face by the light of the street lamp. "You have so much talent. You're smart, you're beautiful. It's a new chapter, girl. And the sooner you realize that, the better off you will be. So go on up to Mayberry." Eugenia smiled and looked at Sophia, who kept talking. "Go find yourself a man, get laid, if you want to, have fun and come back here ready to conquer the world. Or maybe conquer it up there. The possibilities are endless. You just never know what's around that next corner."

Eugenia managed to smile. *Maybe she's right. You really never know what's around that next corner.*

Chapter 3

Maine or Bust

Eugenia loaded the last suitcase in her RAV4 SUV, climbed into her vehicle and headed up the road at the ungodly hour of 4 a.m. on Monday. Her route was mapped out for her using the old-school Triple A trip tick, although she did have a GPS. She stopped by 7-Eleven to get an extra-large coffee and headed onto I-95 North.

She had called her Aunt Nell the day before to let her know that she was leaving the next day.

"I would come with you but my ankle is still bothering me, since I sprained it," she stated.

"Are you sure you don't want me to come by and take care of you?" added Eugenia. "I ain't working."

"No girl, you know I'm at your Aunt Tess's house." Eugenia forgot that she called Aunt Nell's cell phone. Aunt Nell continued, "She's getting on my nerves but she makes a great chicken soup, so it's all good. You need to go up to the cottage and spend some time up there. I think your dad left some stuff up there for you to see. It might interest you."

"Like what?" asked Eugenia.

"Not really sure. With that crazy-ass brother of mine, who knows. He was always digging around and asking questions. I guess you'll have to wait till you get there. You drive safely and call me when you arrive."

"Okay. Thanks, Aunt Nell. Love ya."

"Love ya, baby. Take care."

And they both hung up.

Eugenia listened to a comedy channel on her satellite radio and found herself nearly choking as she laughed while Wanda Sykes presented her own brand of comedy as Eugenia crossed the Piscataqua River Bridge, entering the state of Maine. She drove a few more hours, hitting several towns along the way because at this point in her travels, she had to leave interstate 95 and travel on Route 1. She couldn't help but stop in a few places and take some pictures of the beauty that the great state of Maine had to offer. The humidity had left the air and it was crisp, feeling almost spring-like.

It was around four in the afternoon when she drove into Camden, and Eugenia was ready for bed. After driving through the historic downtown district, she made a right turn at the Camden Public Library and could see the Camden Harbor on the right with its dozens of boats of all shapes and sizes. She continued up a slight hill, made another right and the cottage came into view.

The small wooden white cottage was located on a tree-lined street that contained an eclectic mix of housing styles—some were multi-family homes, as noted by the several mail boxes standing outside of the homes. Others were single-family homes. Some had rather large porches. She pulled up to the cottage on the left side, parked out front and got out. She stood there for a few minutes, taking in the beauty of the neighborhood and the large trees that provided shade. The memories were coming back to her and familiarity set in. She could certainly understand why her father bought such a home nestled in this part of the country. But why Maine? What was the connection to this beautiful, picturesque town? Was it something to do with her mom? Why here? For some odd reason, Eugenia was all of a sudden curious about this place.

Sometimes you really have to step back and look at things. With the way that bank was running me ragged at times, I didn't have time to think and wonder about stuff like this, she thought.

Eugenia walked down the path to the cottage, ascended the three steps onto the small, wooden porch, unlocked the door and entered. As she entered the small foyer, she stepped into the living room and stood there for a few minutes, taking in the décor. The afternoon sunlight streamed in through the numerous windows and just lit up the room. It looked pretty much the way it was when she was last there. The room had a nautical theme, appropriate for this seaside town. The walls were decorated with various photographs of ships. There were several pictures of a lighthouse and the captions read, "Curtis Island Light".

I guess dad liked this lighthouse for some reason. He has enough pictures, from every angle, Eugenia observed.

The color theme was mahogany brown and teal. There were seashells on the coffee and end tables, fishermen's nets decorated the walls, pictures of her dad and mom on the fireplace mantel. There were several pictures of Eugenia and her dad and of Eugenia by herself. She remembered all of those pictures.

Walking over to her dad's bedroom, Eugenia hesitantly opened the door. She entered and stood there for a few minutes. Her father's scent still lingered in the air. All of the windows were still closed but the caretakers hired by her father had done a good job maintaining the house. Eugenia slowly walked around the room. The queen size, four-poster bed was neatly made. She opened the closets and saw only what looked like a photo album occupying the top shelf. She sat on the bed, taking everything in and, for some odd reason, didn't cry. Eugenia just basked in the memories and a smile even appeared on her face as she recalled the wonderful dad that he was. After sitting for a few more minutes, Eugenia got up and left the room, closing the door behind her.

She then went to her room and opened the door. It looked pretty much the same as she remembered; not a typical 15-year-old's room in that there were no posters lining the walls, or stuffed animals on the shelves. It consisted of the usual bedroom furnishings: dresser, chest of drawers and a queen size bed.

Eugenia walked through the kitchen, unlocked the back door and went out onto the steps leading to the backyard. From the steps, she glanced out into the small backyard framed by mature oak, pine, and poplar trees that provided shade. The grass was freshly cut and there were a few hydrangea bushes blooming in colors of pink, white and blue dotting the backyard landscape. Various types of birds darted from tree to tree and their chirping filled the air. She took in the beauty. *I've never had a backyard,* she thought, having only owned a condo. Eugenia took a breath, exhaled, and stood there for a few minutes enjoying the beauty of the yard.

The initial introduction to the cottage wasn't as bad as Eugenia thought it would be. Instead of feeling sad and depressed at being back here without her dad, Eugenia felt a certain odd level of safety. She felt secure and loved, to have been loved and had such a wonderful father. Perhaps that's what made her feel this amount of security.

Eugenia couldn't decide if she was hungry or tired. She settled on hunger and ventured out to the supermarket that she had passed on the way in to buy some food for the next few days. After arriving at the market, as she was inspecting the oranges, she heard her cell phone ring. She saw Aunt

Nell's number and remembered that she hadn't called.

"Hello, I'm so sorry, Aunt Nell…"

"Are you there?" Aunt Nell asked.

"Yes, safe and sound. I'm so sorry. I'm in the supermarket just getting a few things."

"As long as you got there okay. How was the drive other than long?"

"Uneventful and long, but pretty. Nice scenery."

"Good. How was the cottage? You okay?"

"Yeah, I wasn't sure that I could go in there, was considering a hotel room. But it was okay, it really was. The caretakers have done a good job. Dad's scent is still there. A lot of memories."

"Good, I was concerned. Well, that's all I need to know. Just wanted to make sure you got there safely. Take care, baby, and call me if you need anything."

"Okay," said Eugenia.

And they both hung up. Eugenia finished her shopping and headed back to the cottage.

The caretakers knew Eugenia was coming so all of the necessary power, refrigerator, water and even the heat and air conditioning were working. She was all set. After Eugenia put everything away, she decided to take a walk by the marina in Camden Bay. Maybe she would treat herself to some Maine chowder since there was a little bit of a chill in the air. She began walking and a woman approached her walking a dog. There was something familiar about the tall white woman with gray hair.

"Eugenia?" called the lady as she got closer.

Eugenia stopped a few feet from her and stared.

"I'm Martha, Martha Turner from next door. Do you remember? Oh, you were probably 14 or 15 the last time I saw you."

Eugenia suddenly remembered Miss Martha.

"Oh my goodness, how are you?" They then hugged while Miss Martha held the dog's leash.

"I've been great. I'm so sorry to hear of your dad. Your Aunt Nell called me. My goodness, you are such a beauty. What do you do now?"

"Well, I was a marketing specialist for a Washington area bank but was recently laid off, due to a buyout. So here I am, on vacation. I just needed a break. You look great, Miss Martha."

"Well, thank you. I hear so much about these mergers and buyouts between these banks. It's really a shame. Well, Henry and I settled up here, deciding to move into our summer home instead of coming up here every summer. He passed away maybe ten years or so ago. I do miss him. So it's just me and Sam," she said pointing to her dog. "But it's nice up here. I miss seeing your dad. He'd be up here pretty much every summer."

"I know. So sorry to hear about Mr. Henry," said Eugenia.

"Thank you. Well, you're looking well. Any husband? Kids?"

"No to either. Was married about 20 years ago but it didn't last. Been into the career and getting my Master's degree."

"Good for you! Yeah, Chuck told me about the philanderer. What a jerk. Better off without him and you look like you have done well. How long are you staying?"

"Two weeks. Then I need to get back and start looking for a job."

"Well, maybe you could move here, have you thought about it? It's peaceful, safe. We hardly lock our doors."

"Oh no, I don't think so. But will come more often."

"Well, I guess it's something to consider. Henry and I moved up here and never regretted it. What's that in your hand?" asking about her laptop.

"Oh, it's a computer. Just going down here to get something to eat, check my emails, look over my résumé. Can you recommend a place to get some chowder?"

"There's a place right down on the water down by the harbor, can't think of the name. But just go to the parking lot," she said pointing the direction of the harbor. "Walk along the sidewalk where all the boats are docked and you'll see seating outside, although it looks as though it's going to rain. Best chowder around, if you ask me."

"Sounds good."

"Well, gotta go now," Miss Martha said as she pulled the dog's leash and walked on down the street towards her house. Then she turned and said, "Eugenia, oh by the way, there's a guy who plays the piano and sings at this restaurant, pretty good voice, too. I think he's the owner. Kinda cute, too," she said winking her eye. Eugenia just smiled.

"See ya later. Come on, Sam."

"Nice seeing you again, Miss Martha. Thanks."

Chapter 4

You Look Wonderful Tonight

E ugenia couldn't believe how much Miss Martha hadn't changed. Except for the white hair and a couple of wrinkles, she was the same tall, lanky woman that she was some 30 years ago. *She's got to be in her nineties. It was great seeing her,* thought Eugenia.

Eugenia arrived at the parking lot by the marina and noticed a waterfall where the Megunticook River meets Camden Bay. The river meanders through the village, making its way under Main Street and ends up cascading over rocks, down a hill, and the rushing water ends up in the bay. Eugenia stood there at the bottom of the falls for a few minutes, marveling at the view and snapping some pictures. What a spectacular sight!

She found the wooden sidewalk that kind of looked like a boardwalk next to the boats in the marina. She passed a hot dog stand with a long line of people waiting. She continued to walk and found the restaurant with an overhang and people seated outside under the roof. She thought she heard the faint sound of someone playing the piano. *This must be the place,* thought Eugenia. The hostess sat her in a room facing the bay occupied by only a few restaurant patrons, and Eugenia peered out the old wooden-framed windows at the multitude of boats. All of a sudden, the clouds opened up, it began to rain and the wind kicked up as well. This forced those restaurant patrons seated outside to pick up their drinks and seek shelter inside the sparsely occupied restaurant.

I swear, is this a Norman Rockwell painting or what? she thought, as she looked out the window. *I wish I knew how to paint. I'd have a ….* Her thoughts were suddenly interrupted by a perky college-aged waitress. Eugenia couldn't help but notice the waitress's flaming red hair, cut short with bangs that practically covered her striking blue eyes. She was clad in a teal-colored t-shirt with Fins, the restaurant's name, sprawled on the front, blue jeans and tennis shoes.

"Good evening, how are you today," she said in a most pleasant tone.

"Great, how are you?"

"Awesome! I'm Megan and will be taking care of you this evening. Can I start you off with a drink?" she asked as she handed Eugenia a menu.

"Nice to meet you, Megan. I'm Eugenia. Yes, I'll have a white wine."

"Pinot Grigio okay?"

"That'll be fine." Eugenia answered as she took the menu.

"Oh, excuse me, Megan." Eugenia said as Megan was walking away; she made an immediate about face.

"Yes?"

"Is this the place where there is a singer playing the piano?"

"Yes, he plays every once in a while." She then looked at her watch. "Probably pretty soon, no set time, though. I think when he gets in the mood."

"Is he the own--...." But before Eugenia could get to the end of the question, Megan was gone. *Well, it looks as though I'm in the right place,* she surmised.

Megan came back with the drink and then asked, "Did you need any more time to look at the menu?"

"I heard the chowder was pretty good."

"The best around," she bragged.

"I'll start off with the chowder then I'll decide what else I want."

"Awesome."

As Eugenia continued to look at the menu, she got her laptop from her carrying case and fired it up. No doubt they had Wi-Fi in here. *Seems every place does nowadays,* she thought.

Megan soon returned with the steaming chowder and some bread and butter to go with it. She continued, "Did you decide what you wanted?"

"Yes, I'll take this salad with the calamari. That looks good. And some water with a slice of lime."

"Good choice," Megan confirmed. "Be right up. Oh, I think Scott is going to start playing soon. He's the 'piano man'," said Megan with a smirk on her face, no doubt referring to Billy Joel. *Didn't think she'd know anything about that, as young as she is,* thought Eugenia.

Eugenia started on her chowder, which was awesome, as Megan would say. *Wow, this is good.*

Eugenia's signed into her laptop and began looking at her resume, reviewing it to see if she needed to change anything. She then went to her LinkedIn account to see what needed updating. As she took another spoonful of her chowder, Eugenia could faintly hear the keys from the piano. She really didn't pay much attention at first, engrossed in making her LinkedIn profile look as good as possible. But she couldn't help but notice the song being played, "All I Ask of You."

I think that's from The Phantom of the Opera soundtrack, thought Eugenia. *Wow, he's pretty good* and Eugenia found herself not concentrating so much on the laptop but listening to the music. The gentle tune made her lose focus and she found herself staring out at the boats in the marina. *What a sight,* she thought and ate a piece of the warm bread.

Moving here, staying here? She began to reflect on the words Miss Martha said to her earlier and thought of the possibility. She'd probably be one of the few blacks here. *I ain't seen any yet—not one black face!* Eugenia thought. Eugenia found herself looking less at her laptop and focusing more on the wetness that the brief shower created outside of the window. The brief shower had ceased and the evening sun began to show through a few lingering clouds. All that was left of the shower was the rain drops that dripped outside the wooden-framed windows and that fresh rain smell. The beautiful melodic tune continued only to come to an end. Eugenia's focus was no longer on the laptop, just on the sights and smells of Camden, Maine.

"How's the chowder?" said a male voice, startling Eugenia. She looked up to see a bearded, dark-haired man who stood in front of her, so tall that she had to tilt her head back a bit to see his handsome face. His nearly shoulder-length, dark brown hair was a bit tussled as it fell around his face. He wore glasses, brown herringbone patterned with plastic frames, kind of a round shape. She noticed his bright brown eyes behind the glasses seemed to sparkle, or maybe that was the effect of the wine. He had a pleasant, warm, comforting smile that created crow's feet in the corner of his eyes.

"It's really great," Eugenia answered, smiling back at him.

"Hi, I'm Scott Mackey, part owner of this fine establishment," he bragged.

"It's nice to meet you, Scott. Are you the piano man?"

"Guilty as charged," he answered. "My two partners and I bought this restaurant a few years ago. Always wanted to be a lounge singer, probably was one in my former life. So I made good use of those piano lessons I took as a kid and I entertain the patrons." He then paused. "I've never seen you here before. Are you here for the Lobster Fest?"

"Yes, kind of. I'm Eugenia Watts. My dad owns a cabin right over there." She pointed towards the marina. "Just came up for a couple of weeks for vacation." Eugenia didn't want to go into the gory details of the layoff.

"Oh, my God, are you related to Chuck Watts? I see a slight resemblance."

"Yes, guilty as charge." *Dad appeared to be pretty well known in these parts.* "I'm his daughter."

"It is so great to meet you! I'm sorry to hear of his passing. Great guy!"

"Thank you. He came here?"

"Oh, yes, well, since I've been here which has been a little more than three years. Yes, he loved the chowder."

Eugenia looked out of the window for a second and Scott noticed the expression change on her face, with the reminder of her father's passing.

"Well, I'm going to make my rounds. That's what any good restaurant owner does, right?" Eugenia looked up at him and smiled. "It was such a pleasure meeting you, Eugenia. That's a pretty name."

For a pretty woman, Scott thought but stopped himself from saying it. He didn't want to leave but thought it was too presumptuous and unprofessional to ask if he could join her. Eugenia hadn't noticed but when he first entered the room, his eyes scanned the open space, and he was immediately drawn to her. He had hurriedly made his rounds and greeted the customers more quickly than usual, so that he could swiftly make his way to the corner table where he noticed this beautiful African American woman staring at her laptop. She sat there looking stunning in her blue jeans and pink tank top. Her hair was parted on the left side and her straight hair ended at her shoulder and was curled under, the other side was tucked behind her ear. She sat with one leg crossed over the other, looking outside at the brief shower.

"Thank you," as she thanked him for the compliment. "It was nice meeting you as well."

"Will you be coming back soon?" Scott felt at this point that he had stepped out of line. But he couldn't process the fact that he may never see her again…and he wanted to.

Eugenia looked up again, a little surprised at the question, but, nevertheless answered, "Yes."

He smiled, left her table and continued to greet the other guests. He occasionally glanced over at Eugenia and noticed her salad had come. Scott then left the room and went back to the piano.

Eugenia was eating the delicious calamari salad and heard the piano again. As she researched a company that interested her, her attention turned to the song that was playing and she recognized the tune as an instrumental version of "Wonderful Tonight" by Eric Clapton. She began to think about some of the words. The song tells of a man and a woman getting ready to leave to attend a party. The man compliments the woman on how beautiful she looks, while she is applying her makeup and brushing her hair. *Okay, this can't be happening*, thought Eugenia. *If I wasn't a sensible, level headed woman, I'd think he was playing this song for me. Nah. This is crazy!*

She then shook it off, finished her meal and asked Megan for the check. As Eugenia left the restaurant, she glanced over at the piano that sat empty. It was dusk by now and the streetlights of the town began to come on. She proceeded up a narrow, slight incline passageway to Main Street, walking briefly up towards the library that sat on the corner. She had seen it earlier as she began to remember landmarks from when she first arrived in town. She made that right turn onto Atlantic Avenue and continued the four or five block walk to Sea Street.

Turning onto her street, she spotted Miss Martha sitting in an Adirondack chair on her porch.

"Hello, again. Did you go to the restaurant to see the piano man?"

Eugenia stopped at the sound of her voice and stood in the street in front of Miss Martha's porch.

"Yes, I did."

"Is he cute or what? Reminds me of Josh Groban, that cute singer."

"He really does. I couldn't think who he resembled. You're right."

"Did he sing? Got a beautiful voice."

"No, he didn't. Just played instrumentals."

"Too bad. You'll have to go there again."

"I intend to," Eugenia answered, with a little bit of a smirk. "He asked if I was coming back. Kind of took me aback a little. Then he played that song by Eric Clapton, 'Wonderful Tonight.'"

Miss Martha looked up as if trying to recall. "Oh yeah, I remember that." Then a smile came onto her face. "Do you think he was playing that song with you in mind? Of all the songs that he could play, he picked that one," she said with a wink. "After all, you do look wonderful tonight."

In the light of the streetlamp, Miss Martha couldn't see Eugenia blush. "Why thank you, Miss Martha. But that's silly. Come on!"

"Hey, stranger things have happened!"

"Okay, with that thought, I'm getting on in here for the night. You have a good evening, Miss Martha."

"You too, dear. Nice to have you here."

"Nice to be here," Eugenia answered sincerely.

After Scott played the Eric Clapton song, he retreated to his office to do some paperwork. He sat at the window in his corner office and glanced out to see Eugenia exit the restaurant. *Maybe I should walk her home.* He knew she didn't live that far away; he knew where Chuck lived. But he didn't want to jump the gun. *I hope she'll return.* He watched the way her hair blew in the slight breeze as she walked, her jeans that fitted her perfectly as she adjusted the laptop case on her shoulder. He watched her until she got out of sight.

Hopefully she liked the song. It was for her, he thought.

Chapter 5

Scott

Eugenia was used to waking up around 5:30 to go to work and that habit was hard to break. She rose and fixed herself a cup of coffee before venturing out for her morning walk. Only a few people were out and she was grateful for the solitude. She tried to keep a good pace but found herself slowing down a bit to check out the new surroundings. She spotted Scott's restaurant in the distance, as she peered from the vantage point of Atlantic Avenue, looking into Camden Harbor. *Gosh, he couldn't have a better location. I wonder how much that cost him.* She continued her walk that lasted about 45 minutes and headed back to the cottage.

After her shower and breakfast, she continued her unpacking and began her daily online search for jobs. By the afternoon, Eugenia decided that she had enough of the job search and began to explore the cottage a bit more. Even though the caretakers had done a great job with keeping the place clean, she did some minor touch-ups just to get it the way she wanted it. She opened all of the windows to let the fresh air in. The fresh cool Maine air was a welcomed addition.

Eugenia wanted to explore the photo album in her dad's closet. Gnawing questions still bothered her—why did her dad buy this place and why here in Camden, Maine? And what is it with all these pictures of the Curtis Island Lighthouse? She thought she'd start by retrieving this overstuffed book from her dad's room.

Opening the photo album/scrap book combination, Eugenia began to read what was there. There were newspaper articles, some photos and many hand-written notes by her father. She started from the beginning.

The notes seemed to center on the Curtis Island Lighthouse, which is on the small island out in Camden Harbor, and there were notes of the history of the Town of Camden. The island was named for Cyrus Curtis in 1934 but before that it was named Negro Island. *Wow, this is interesting,* thought Eugenia as she continued to read. In 1769, early European settlers began moving into the area. She continued to read about the history and then came upon this: one man by the name of James Davis came here with his wife. He had an African cook who saw the five-acre island and said that this was his island. So up until 1934, it was named Negro Island. *Hmm*

She leafed through the book continuing to read. In 1834, Congress set aside $4,500 to build the lighthouse. It was subsequently finished in 1836 and named Negro Island Light.

The material chronicled when the residence or keeper's house on the island was built, the names of the lighthouse keepers and how, in 1970, the residents of Camden convinced the Coast Guard to turn the light station over to the town; that's the status today. Eugenia continued reading all the facts and figures about the island and the lighthouse until she could read no more. She hadn't noticed that a few hours had flown by and that she was getting hungry. It was nearly time for dinner.

She bought enough food for about a week and went to her kitchen to rustle up something. *That chowder was really good yesterday,* she thought, as she peered into her refrigerator. And in an instant she was out the door with her laptop case on her shoulder so she could continue her job search and check her emails, neither of which she had done today. *I wouldn't mind hearing some piano playing,* she thought

It was Tuesday, a little early in the evening and the restaurant wasn't crowded. She requested to sit at the same table, so that she could enjoy the view of the marina, and settled in, firing up the laptop.

"Hey, you're back." It was Megan again, perky as ever.

"Hey, how are you?" *I hope she doesn't think I'm some horny old woman after Scott. He was cute, though. I hope it's not too obvious. I could use some guy serenading me with a piano. That's never happened to me before. I'm leaving here in a couple of weeks, so what the fuck!*

"I am awesome. Can I start you off with a drink?"

"I'll take a Malibu Sunrise, please."

"Awesome."

Eugenia was checking her emails when she heard the piano once again. The tune was an instrumental, not a sad song, just a pleasant tune. She didn't know the name of it, but it was a calming piano piece that had a somewhat upbeat tempo. Yet it was melodic enough that it forced her to turn her attention away from her computer screen and out the window to stare at the beautiful marina. Earlier she had read that this town was one of the most beautiful towns in Maine—in all of Maine! Some article described Camden as the place "where the mountains meet the sea." *In Maryland, we have mountains and we have the Atlantic Ocean—but they're more than an hour's drive in between them.* Eugenia saw Mt. Battie sitting off in the distance. *It was kind of the background for the town, making up a horizon, sort of speak.*

Megan brought back the drink and Eugenia ordered what she came there for—the chowder. She then ordered a club sandwich and a small salad. As she sipped her drink, a familiar tune was being played on the piano— "Truly" by Lionel Ritchie. This time Scott was singing. *Wow.*

Eugenia then stood up and walked over just enough to see him. *Good he has his back to me,* she thought. *He really does have a beautiful voice.* She stood there almost mesmerized and surprised that he had such a nice voice. When the song ended, she watched him stand up, his back still facing her direction. She noticed his jeans, burgundy t-shirt, that he hadn't bothered to tuck into his pants. The shirt had the name of the restaurant advertised on the back. She watched him and, as soon as she suspected that he was going to turn around, she ducked back to her table, hoping he didn't see her.

Scott began making his rounds, greeting the customers and, once again, as Eugenia took a sip of her chowder, he appeared in front of her, greeting her with that smile.

"Eugenia." *He remembered my name,* she thought.

"Hello, how are you? Scott, right?"

"Yes."

"As you can see I'm back for the chowder."

"Excellent choice. It's nice seeing you, again. How's everything going?"

"Great."

"How's the vacation?"

"Not bad at all. This town is so beautiful!" exclaimed Eugenia.

"It's got to be one of the most beautiful places I've ever seen, not that I've been to too many places, but it's pretty awesome."

"Were you playing the piano earlier?"

"Guilty once again. Did you like it?"

"Yes, very much so. What was that instrumental piece that you were playing?"

Good, she liked it, Scott thought. "It's called…. Uh, do you mind if I sit, unless this seat is taken."

"Yes, I mean, no, I don't mind if you sit," *Did he think someone was joining me? And can I stumble over my words anymore?* Of the four seats at the table, he sat down in the one closest to Eugenia, facing her, crossing the ankle of his long leg over his knee. His tussled dark brown hair framed his face and his beard was neatly trimmed. She noticed a few gray hairs in his beard. *Nice.*

"The song was called 'Life is Grand.' I think it's referring to the grand piano. The artist is called Silvard."

"It was beautiful. And was that you singing Lionel Ritchie?"

"Yes. I told you I am a closet lounge singer," Scott said with a smile.

"You're very good."

"Thank you so much. So what have you been doing while on vacation?" He seemed not to want to get up and make his rounds, getting into an easy, comfortable position in the wooden chair. Eugenia didn't mind, not a bit. Her drink was finished and she was feeling the effects a little. She ordered water for the rest of the meal, wanting to keep her wits about her.

"Well, I lost, was displaced, at my job back in Maryland. In other words, laid off. So, with the help of my handy, dandy laptop, I am looking, oh, wait a minute, am exploring my options. At the placement service that I've been working with, they told us to say that. I got a nice severance package as a result and I had planned on taking this vacation for quite a while, before my unfortunate layoff. So, here I am." Scott smiled at Eugenia's attitude.

"What did you do?"

"I was a marketing specialist at a bank over 20 years."

"Wow," said Scott no doubt empathetic at the time she had put in at her job before the layoff.

"The bank was subsequently bought out and all of us dinosaurs, most of us had at least 15 years, were offered either a part-time position or a severance package. Since I couldn't afford to work part-time, I took the package. We kind of saw the writing on the wall at some point. This vacation is helping put some distance between me and Maryland and I feel like I can figure things out a little more clearly. I'm so glad dad bought this cottage. I wished I had come up with him more often."

Scott then interjected. "Yeah, I think as we get into adulthood, we're so wrapped up in our lives, spending time with parents seems an afterthought. You're from the D.C. area, right?"

"Yes."

"Yeah, that's right, Chuck was from D.C. Where abouts?"

"From Silver Spring."

"I'm from D.C.!"

"Really?" said Eugenia

"Yes, Northwest. Wow, what a coincidence. Where did you go to high school? College?"

"Montgomery Blair, then the University of Maryland. What about you? High School? College?" asked Eugenia.

"Gonzaga, then went on to Catholic University. Majored in Business Administration."

"What was your concentration?" *I feel like I'm stopping him from his job. I guess he's okay with this,* thought Eugenia.

"Management. I worked for the government a few years. My ex-wife, daughter and I would come up here to Lobster Fest and I fell in love with the area. At some point in the marriage we grew apart and after our daughter was old enough, not a young child, we divorced. She's in college at your alma mater, the University of Maryland. She's 20."

Eugenia was trying to process the information and at the same time felt guilty about holding him up from his rounds.

"You don't look old enough to have a 20-year-old," she complimented him.

"Well, thank you. Yes, and she's the apple of my eye, needless to say."

Someone from the kitchen area was calling him. Scott then stood up, looking towards the kitchen area and said, "Well, they're calling. Look, Eugenia, can I call you later? We close at nine; I can probably call you a little before that. I'd like to continue this conversation," he said with sincerity.

And with a little bit of a surprise, Eugenia asked, "May I call you, say around 9:00? If you're busy, I can call you back. Is that okay?"

"Yes, that would be great! I'd like that," he said, as he looked at her and winked. Eugenia couldn't help but smile. He reached into his front pocket, pulled out a business card to give to her.

"I'll talk to you later," as he turned and rushed off to the kitchen.

Eugenia then put his number into her phone. She continued with her meal, processing the conversation that just occurred. Once finished, she paid her check, packed up the laptop and left the restaurant. As she left, she glanced over at the piano that sat silent. He must still be in the kitchen.

Dusk had settled over the town. Who is this handsome stranger? Who is this person whom she seems to feel at ease with so soon? Who is this white guy that she is so attracted to, completely out of her element? Well, not completely—she dated one or two white guys and has always had white friends. Growing up in Silver Spring, Md., you couldn't help but have white friends. At Montgomery Blair, she was often one of only a few blacks in her classes. Scott seemed really cordial and definitely easy to talk to. As she made her way down Atlantic Avenue and onto Sea Street, she missed Miss Martha on the porch. She must have gone in for the night, as evidenced by the lights on in her house. As Eugenia unlocked her door, she realized she hadn't called Sophia since she'd been here and decided to give her a call

Chapter 6

The Phone Call and Butterflies

H ey girl, what's going on? Hadn't heard from you, thought you might have been kidnapped by some Mainer or catching lobster on some boat. How's it going?" asked Sophia.

Eugenia couldn't help but laugh.

"Girl, you are off the chain. Going well, made it in one piece."

"Well, I know that, see you on Facebook. Pretty place! Found any single lobster men yet, any moose.... uh...people, I don't know. What's up? Been laid yet?"

"Girl, no. I did meet a guy though."

"Great. There's hope for you yet. So, give me the sordid details."

Eugenia described Scott, the restaurant and told her how he played the piano.

"He looks like Josh Groban, the singer, the guy who sings opera?" asked Sophia after Eugenia described him.

"Josh Groban doesn't sing opera. Just not the usual rock stuff that you're always listening to."

"So he looks like Josh Groban, plays the piano and sings. Maybe he's going thru an identity crisis or something?"

"He just favors him a bit. Just had to give you a frame of reference as to what he looks like."

"Okay, so how's that going?" Eugenia told Sophia about his wonderful voice, that he's part owner of the restaurant and everything else she knew so far.

"So he's cute, sings, decent voice. When are you going to make mad passionate love to him?"
"*Sophia!*"

"What? Don't tell me the thought hasn't crossed your mind? You're only going to be there two weeks. You could have sex with an expiration date!"

"Sophia, look, he's cute, yes. And he can sing. I'm too old for that shit. I decided a long time ago that being somebody's lover or one-night stand is not for me. After my divorce from the asshole of a husband that I had, it seemed like every guy I dated wanted a couple of women, just like the asshole. I'm tired of the games, the no commitment freaks! Besides, it's so romantic when he sings. It's kind of nice, kind of fairy tale-like. Do you know what he sang last night after meeting me?"

"What?"

"Well, he was greeting the customers, you know how restaurant owners do, making sure the food is okay. So he came over to my table, continuing to make his rounds and we spoke for a few minutes. He introduced himself and everything. He then went back to the piano and he played an instrumental version of that Eric Clapton song 'Wonderful Tonight'. Isn't that something?"

"And you think he was playing it to you? Please, Eugenia. That shit only happens in the movies."

"Sophia, when did you get so cynical? Don't you believe in romance? Don't you think there is a possibility that someone can be that romantic?"

"Shit no!"

"*Sophia!*" Eugenia said sternly.

"Eugenia, maybe. Geez, I don't know. Maybe I'm just a realist. You know… whatever! You go ahead and have your fun. But if I were you, I'd be having mad, passionate sex with him and getting the heck back to reality. But you do your thing. Just have fun. You deserve that."

"Thanks, Sophia. Look, I'm really tired of the games, I really am. At this point in my life, I want it all, the romance, somebody who wants to commit, someone who really loves me. And I'm not settling for less. Do you know what I mean?"

"Yeah, I do. I know what you mean, girl."

They went on to talk about the cottage, Chuck and Miss Martha. Eugenia said how well the caretakers had maintained the cottage.

"Well, let me go now. I have to call Scott at around nine. I promised I would." They went on to talk about the conversation and that she was calling him. They then said their goodbyes and hung up.

It had gotten dark since she got home, so Eugenia turned on some more lights. She went into the kitchen, retrieved a bottle of wine from the refrigerator. After pouring herself a glass and grabbing her phone, she went out on the small front porch to curl up in the rocking chair and dialed Scott's number. She could feel butterflies in her stomach as the phone rang, once, twice… "Hello"

"Hello, Scott?"

"Eugenia, how are you? You made it home okay. I'm assuming you are at home?"

"Yes, safe and sound. Is this a bad time?"

"No, not at all. Actually I left early so I'm just getting in the door. Hold on for a second…just let me get this door, turn these lights on so I won't hurt myself in my own home. Okay, that's better. Let me grab this beer…" Eugenia heard what sounded like a refrigerator shut. "Ok I'm all yours, sort of speak. Now where were we in our conversation?"

"We were talking about the apple of your eye, your daughter."

"Oh, yeah. Chloe. Yeah, she's at the University of Maryland majoring in accounting. Smart kid, like her mom. Don't see her as much as I'd like to. How about you? Are you married? Kids? You're not married, are you?"

"No to both."

"I guess I should have asked before now."

"Was married about 20 years ago. We weren't married long, three years or so. No kids. We met in college, first love and stuff."

"Twenty years ago? *How old are you?* Oh my God, did I really say that? Eugenia, I'm sorry. It's just that I thought you were maybe in your 30s. I'm sitting here doing the math and thinking child bride at 10!"

Eugenia just laughed. "It's okay," still laughing. "Thanks for the compliment. I don't mind—I'm 45."

"*So am I!* We have so much in common. We're both from the D.C. area. We're both the same age. Don't tell me you love piña coladas, getting caught in the rain?" No doubt referencing a hit song from the 1970s.

Eugenia couldn't help but laugh.

"Just a little humor there…very little right, I guess?"

"You really got jokes tonight, huh."

"Yeah, I guess. I'm usually not this silly," explained Scott.

"On a more serious note, how did you know my father?"

"Just from coming into the restaurant. I think he told me where he lived, where his cottage was. I knew he had a daughter and that he had lost his wife some years ago. Of course, we both were from the D.C. area, so we hit it off pretty quickly. So when he came into town on vacation, he'd come by and give me the lowdown of what was going on back home. That's all I remember. Sometimes he called me 'DC'. Yeah, good guy."

There was some silence as Eugenia processed and then Scott broke the silence.

"Hey, Eugenia, have you ever been to Lobster Fest?"

"No, I had planned on going while I'm here."

"Would you like to go with me?"

Dead silence.

"If you want. I'd like to take you," asked Scott again, not expecting this silence and not knowing what to think of it. *Gosh, what's going on?* he thought.

"Yes. Sorry for the hesitation. Yes, that would be nice," Eugenia finally answered.

"Great! What about tomorrow evening, say around 5-ish? I could come and pick you up or we could meet somewhere in town. It's up to you," Scott said trying to gauge her feelings.

"You could come by here and pick me up. You know where I live, right?"

"Yes."

"I'll be ready at five. Oh, by the way, where do you live?" asked Eugenia.

"Off of Mechanic Street. It's not far from downtown Camden. I could show you tomorrow on the way to the fest. We'll do a drive-by…Uh, sorry, these jokes just keep coming."

Eugenia laughed once more and said, "Okay, that sounds good."

"Eugenia, what's the origin of your name? You were named after someone?"

"It's my maternal grandmother's name. That's what my dad told me. I've never met her; she died before I was born."

"Oh, you know what? Chuck mentioned something about your mother and he was doing some research on your mother's side. Your mother told him that there was some connection with her family and this town. That's what brought him here. Did he ever say anything like that to you?"

Puzzled, Eugenia said, "No, he didn't. But there are several pictures of this Curtis Island Lighthouse on the walls in the cottage. There's a painting, several photographs, they're all over the place. Don't know where they came from."

"Wow. That's interesting. Sounds like a mystery. When you said that you were named after your maternal grandmother, that made me think of…" Scott hesitated, but continued, "Well, it was one of the last conversations that I had with him."

"Yeah. Well, I appreciate you telling me. And if you remember something more, let me know. I've been looking through a scrapbook that was in his closet and it has newspaper articles, some photos and some history about the town. It's interesting, to say the least. I think I'll continue looking tomorrow."

"Oh, another thing. Do you know where the library is?" asked Scott.

"Oh yeah, I remember passing it on the way in. It's right up on the corner."

"Perhaps someone can help you there. I would think they would have quite a bit of info. Don't ask me since I haven't been to a library in years. Plus, it's the coolest building. Check it out!"

"I will, tomorrow. Well, I'm going on to bed. It's getting late," said Eugenia.

"Yeah, it is. Well, thanks so much for calling. I truly enjoyed talking to you and I'm looking forward to seeing you tomorrow. I'll try to keep the corny jokes to a minimum."

"It's okay.... I like corny," said Eugenia.

"You're just saying that to spare me, right?

"No...not really."

"Okay. Well, good night. I hope you sleep well," said Scott.

"Goodnight."

They both hung up. *Oh, thank God I'm home because this wine is making me drunk. Whoa,* she thought. *He really seems sweet. Tomorrow should be fun.*

Eugenia went inside, locked the door and got ready for bed.

Chapter 7

The Camden Public Library

Eugenia got up at her regular hour and walked in a different direction from the day before. After her walk, she showered and ate breakfast before gathering up the scrapbook and heading the short distance to the Camden Public Library. Entering on the Atlantic Avenue entrance, which appeared to be underground, Eugenia was completely taken aback by the uniqueness of this building. Before asking the librarian any questions about the contents of her scrapbook, she inquired about the building.

"Yes, you are currently in the basement. If you go up the stairs to the first floor, you're in the original building. The first and second floors are part of the original library, and they built a basement to expand the building. It is truly unique in that what's above us is the lawn of the original building."

Eugenia added, "It looks as though this part was built out of the side of a mountain."

"It was," she answered.

"This is the coolest building I've ever seen. Wow."

"We get that a lot. It's a great place to work, also. Well, I see that you have quite a scrapbook there. How may I help you?" asked the librarian.

Eugenia showed her the scrapbook with all its contents and the librarian immediately explained, "In the first floor history section there is a lady who is quite knowledgeable about Camden's history. I believe she is there now. You may go up the stairs or there's an elevator right next to the stairs."

"Okay. Thank you so much," said Eugenia.

"You're welcome and good luck. Looks interesting," she said enthusiastically.

Approaching the stairs, Eugenia looked at the various pictures lining the walls in the hallway. There were pictures and some biographical information about Edna St. Vincent Millay, the author, who was born in nearby Rockland and spent time in Camden. The hall also contained glass display cases and one especially attracted Eugenia's attention. As she peered into the glass case, she noticed the reference to Negro Island Light and began reading the text. It was pretty much the same information that she had read before in the scrapbook. *Hmmm,* she thought.

She ascended the stairs and turned left to go into a large room that contained an assortment of books, magazines and various publications about Camden and other area locations. Somewhat hidden from the entrance sat a dark haired, white woman probably in her mid-thirties. She sat staring at a computer screen but looked up when she spotted Eugenia, who was smiling and walking in her direction. The woman immediately rose to her feet and acknowledged Eugenia while looking with curious eyes at Eugenia's scrapbook.

"Good morning," greeted Eugenia.

"Good morning. And how are you today?"

"Great. I was wondering if I may ask you a couple of questions."

"Yes, I see that you have quite a handsome book there."

"Yes." Eugenia sat the book on the counter that separated the two women and began by showing her some of the articles, photos and various scrap pieces of paper.

"My dad owned a cottage up on Sea Street and I'm staying there for a couple of weeks. I found this book in a closet and am curious as to why he had so much information about the Curtis Island Lighthouse. The cottage has photos and paintings all over the place. Just kind of curious."

"Let me take a look." She looked through some of the paperwork. "Your father, is his name Chuck?"

"Yes, did you know him?"

"Well, I met him maybe last summer. He came here asking about the lighthouse. Not really sure why. I just figured he liked it. It's beautiful, I must say. I let him know that it was once called Negro Island Light. I got the impression that he may have some connection to it, but he never said that he did."

"Well, I also found this list of names." Eugenia showed her the list that was hand-written in cursive, containing the following names

> Eugenia Potts (Freeman)
> Martha Freeman (Bailey)
> Eugenia Bailey (Anderson)
> Margaret Anderson (Pratt)
> Eugenia Pratt (Monroe)
> Gayle Monroe (Watts)

"Do you know any of these women?"

"Well, the first name, Gayle, is my mom and Monroe is her maiden name and Watts is her married name. The second is my grandmother, of whom I was named. I had heard that her husband's name was George. The rest I don't recognize."

The librarian looked at the list. "Eugenia is listed quite a few times. And you don't recognize the other women?"

"No."

"Do you have any relatives on your mother's side whom you can ask?"

"Not that I know of. My mom was an only child, born in D.C. Her parents have been long gone as well as most of her side of the family, at least the ones that I know of."

"Do you think that these women may be somehow related to you? I mean, Eugenia is so common in this group. It really would be a good assumption." The librarian paused for a few seconds then continued. "Are you familiar with the U.S. Census records?"

"Well, yes. I know it's taken every 10 years. Why?"

"Well, we have access online to the census and the records contain so much information. It's a good place to start researching your ancestors. I'd be glad to show you."

"That would be great."

"When was your mother born?"

"1949."

"Well, the most recent census that was made public was the 1940 census and it became available in 2012. Census records are available to the public every 72 years. So, she would not be in the 1940, but your grandmother, her mother, would be."

She directed Eugenia over to the computer and she went to an online database. After bringing up the 1940 census, she asked Eugenia for information about her grandmother such as where she was born, when she was born, where she might have lived in 1940, etc. After some searching through several files, they came upon a possible match.

"Monroe was your mother's maiden name?" she asked.

"Yes."

"I wonder if these are all maiden names, the names not in parenthesis," she pondered referring to the list. "That would be great if that was so."

"Why is that so great?"

"It can be a challenge when doing research on one's ancestors if all you have is a woman's married name. It looks as though you have both maiden and their married surnames listed here."

"Oh."

"I'm going to assume that these are the women's maiden names and their married names are in parenthesis, since your mother is listed that way." Eugenia searched while the librarian looked over her shoulder. They then came upon a Eugenia Pratt, 11 years old, living in D.C. and the daughter of Samuel and Margaret Pratt.

"Would you say she was born in the late 1920s, being that your mom was born in 1949? That's a good possibility. They'd be about 20 years apart," said the librarian.

"Yeah, that is a good possibility."

"Let's look at this census record a little more closely to see who else was living in the household."

They both looked at the cursive writing in the document and read the information.

"Oh my goodness—look at this. The record has Samuel Pratt as head of household, and the other people listed are his wife, Margaret and his mother-in-law, *Eugenia Anderson*. The fourth person on your list is Eugenia Bailey (Anderson). I think we have a match."

It took a few minutes for Eugenia to process this information. She then took out her notebook and took notes just to get it straight in her head. *It looks as though these might be my ancestors*, she thought. *This is really interesting.*

"You look like you got the hang of this so I'm going to leave you here to explore. Let me know if you need any help. Wow, this is fascinating."

Before leaving, the librarian suggested that Eugenia draw a pedigree chart starting with herself, then her parents, grandparents and recommended just to research her mother's side since she had the listing of women and probably their maiden and married surnames. The "map" would help to figure out what path to take.

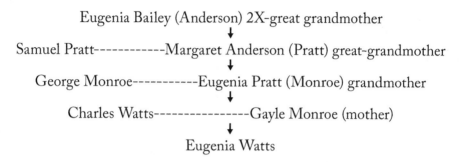

Eugenia Bailey (Anderson) 2X-great grandmother
↓
Samuel Pratt------------Margaret Anderson (Pratt) great-grandmother
↓
George Monroe----------Eugenia Pratt (Monroe) grandmother
↓
Charles Watts---------------Gayle Monroe (mother)
↓
Eugenia Watts

After drawing the chart, Eugenia decided to concentrate on the 1940s census records before her and find more information about her grandmother, Eugenia Pratt Monroe.

• She found the street address, including the house number of her great-grandparents in Northwest D.C.
• They rented their home.
• Both Samuel and Margaret Pratt graduated from high school.
• Samuel Pratt was a chauffeur and Margaret was a domestic.
• Margaret's mother, Eugenia Anderson, was a widow.

Eugenia printed out a blank 1940s census form and hand-wrote all the information written in cursive on the census form using a pencil at the advice of the librarian. She also put the current date as per the advice of the librarian, whose name was Jean. Eugenia stopped and stared at the information that she had collected. Looking at her watch, she realized the time had flown and decided that this was all the research she was going to do today.

Thanking Jean and promising to return tomorrow, Eugenia gathered all her things and headed back to her cottage. As she walked up Atlantic Avenue, she realized that, yes this was her cottage. Her dad had left it to her and all she had to pay were the taxes—it was free and clear of a mortgage. As she walked home, she began to wonder about the possibility of making this her home, escaping the rat race of the D.C. suburbs, the traffic – oh my God, the traffic -- the crime, the craziness. It was so peaceful here. *But there aren't any black folks!* she thought. Not that she's ever had any problem with getting along with whites. No, never been an issue.

And this guy I'm going out with? You know what, I'm not going to think about this too much. Just go with the flow, ride it out. See what happens. A piano playing, restaurant owner? Geez! He's cute, though!

Let me get my ass in this house, figure out what I'm going to wear, fix my hair. Oh my goodness! How am I going to get my hair done being up here in Mayberry?

Lemme get ready for this evening. Five o'clock will be here before I know it.

Chapter 8

The Maine Lobster Fest

Eugenia decided to wear a pair of denim shorts with a denim sleeveless blouse and pulled her hair into a ponytail, tied with a scarf. Her earrings were large gold hoops and she wore sandals. A small, 14-carat gold choker chain adorned her neck. Taking one last look at the mirror in her bedroom, she decided that everything looked good. She smoothed on sunscreen because black people can get sunburn, especially one with her light copper color complexion.

It was about 4:45 and, as she waited for Scott, Eugenia brought out her research and spread it out on the coffee table, staring at it once again. This information had really made her curious and she found herself enthusiastically anticipating her time in the library tomorrow. While looking at the various pieces of information, she heard a car pull up outside. She peered out the window and saw Scott jump out of his SUV, wearing a pair of plaid shorts with a hem that landed just below his knees, white short-sleeved, V-neck t-shirt, and sandals. He was carrying a bouquet of flowers. *Oh my God. How nice is that?*

Before he could knock on the door, Eugenia immediately opened it as she heard his footsteps on the porch.

"Hey," she said. "How are you?"

"Great. These are for you," as he presented the flowers to Eugenia.

"Oh my goodness, they are so pretty! Thank you so much. Come in."

The beautiful bouquet consisted of pink lilies, white gladiolus, some pink carnations and baby's breath.

"Let me just find something to put these in. Please, make yourself at home." *Wow, can't remember the last time I received flowers,* she thought as she rummaged around the kitchen for a vase, a jar or something in which to put them.

Scott was looking around the living room when she returned from the kitchen with the flowers in a vase and placed them on the fireplace mantel.

"I've seen this cottage many times before but have never been inside. You weren't kidding about the pictures of the Curtis Island Lighthouse. Wow, that's a nice painting! Very pretty," as Scott continued to look around.

"Please sit down," offered Eugenia, pointing to a chair near the coffee table

"What do you have here?" he said as he looked at the contents of the scrapbook laid out on the coffee table.

Eugenia began to tell Scott her time at the library that day, searching for answers to some questions that she had about the scrapbook. He sat back comfortably in the chair, his one long leg crossed over the other one, listening to her and smiling at the things that she had discovered. He found himself almost fascinated by her, noticing her dimples, her beautiful brown eyes and her light copper-colored complexion that was the color of a cup of coffee with maybe two creams. Just beautiful. He was so pleased that he pointed her in the right direction as to where she could get information and was able to help. While listening to her, Scott noticed similarities in her mannerisms as compared to her father. He could definitely see the father and daughter resemblances.

After she finished telling about her day, he let her know the Lobster Fest was a few miles south of Camden in Rockland. With that, Eugenia grabbed her purse and they both headed out the door.

He opened the passenger side and she climbed into the SUV. As Eugenia got into the SUV, she saw Miss Martha sitting on her porch with Sam stretched out on the floor beside her. She told her earlier that she was going out with Scott and Miss Martha was absolutely thrilled. Miss Martha waved and both Scott and Eugenia waved back as they passed her house. They were on their way.

Scott kept his promise and drove by his house. He slowed up a little so that she could get a better look at the two-story frame house, white in color with a porch on the front.

"Very nice. When was it built?"

"1920-something. It's been renovated quite a bit. Got insulation, hardwood floors. I'm buying it and it's really comfortable and has a lot of charm."

"*Is that a motorcycle?*" asked Eugenia, looking at the Honda Gold Wing sitting on the side of the house.

"Yes, that's my toy. You know how guys are, got to have their toys. Have you ever ridden a motorcycle?"

"Yes, a couple of times."

"Maybe you'd like to go for a ride sometimes?" Scott asked.

"That would be nice," she answered, looking over at Scott and smiling. Scott drove back on the main road and continued on Route 1 towards Rockland, going through Rockport, the next town over from Camden.

"You know there's a Rockville, Maine." Scott pointed at the road that led to Rockville, as they stopped at a traffic light. He mentioned that because of the city in Maryland with the same name which they were both familiar.

"So, Eugenia, tell me your life story," said Scott as they passed some bed and breakfast-type hotels located on the side of the road.

"Well, I told you about the layoff. What did you want to know?"

"How was that job and how are you dealing with that?"

"Well, it was my first job after college and I really liked it. It got crazy at times, deadlines to meet, etc. But I loved the people. I was there for 21 years. I miss my co-workers. And how am I dealing with the lay off? Well, I'm okay so far. It's hard but the six months of severance and medical helps. It just means I have a deadline to find a job or I'll have to draw unemployment, which I heard is pretty horrible. So I'm okay. This vacation is doing me a world of good. What about your life story? Family?"

"Well, I have an older sister. It was just the two of us. She's 15 years older than me, so she's 60. My parents, both deceased. My dad was 50 when I was born and my mom was 42. I think I was kind of a surprise. My sister still lives in the D.C. area, over in Alexandria. She has five girls, so I have a bunch of nieces. Very cool, though! My sister pretty much brought me up, since both parents worked. We talk on occasion and I visit whenever I'm in the area. Oh, down this road here." Scott pointed to a road on the left, "There is the coolest lighthouse. It's called the Rockland Breakwater Lighthouse. There's like a mile walkway that is made up of boulders that you have to walk to get to the lighthouse and the home that housed the keepers."
"The keepers?" asked Eugenia.

"Yeah, that's the name for the lighthouse keepers. It's also a name for a lobster that you keep when you have caught a bunch of lobsters and you keep the ones that are the proper size. They measure each lobster that is caught and if the back of the shell is long enough, then it's a keeper, or 'keepa' as the people native to this area pronounce it."

Eugenia laughed at the accent that Scott imitated. She couldn't help but notice how Scott used one of his hands as he spoke and kept the other on the wheel. He would keep his eyes on the road but occasionally look Eugenia's way. He looked great in glasses but Eugenia wondered how he looked without them.

"That's kind of like the people who catch crabs in the Chesapeake Bay. There's a certain size that one can keep and, if it's too small, then they have to throw it back."

"Exactly. I'd like to take you there sometime, if you like," he then said as he stopped at a light and looked over at Eugenia.

"I think that would be nice. I'd like to see it."

"Good."

They continued into Rockland and Scott drove around a bit looking for a parking space. Rockland is a town of about 10,000 residents, Scott explained to Eugenia, but the population swells during Lobster Fest. This year, 2015, marks its 68th year of existence. They found a place to park on the street and walked the short distance to the entry gate. The festival took place in Rockland's Harbor Park and one could see various boats docked in the harbor. One boat docked far out into the harbor stood out; it was the naval ship, the USS Tortuga. Several signs adorned the surrounding bars and restaurants welcoming the service people to the festival and Eugenia noticed many young Marines and sailors walking around amongst the crowds at the festival and on the street.

Eugenia was a bit surprised when Scott took her hand and began showing her the different displays at the festival. He stated that he goes every year. There were vendors selling arts and crafts and, of course, food including chowder, ice cream, and funnel cakes. Several large tents displayed art and a hands-on display where one could pet live sea life such as lobsters, scallops and other sea creatures.

But the most fascinating was the huge lobster steamer. Men with red shirts emblazoned with "Lobster Cooker" brought in huge lobster traps with live lobsters. Wearing rubber gloves, the men put the live lobsters, all wearing bands around their claws, into one of six steamers, and a timer was set. After about 15 minutes, the cooked lobsters came out of the steamer, with their bright red color and were placed into a large plastic container that looked like a cooler, but it in reality was a covered insulated container that would hold the heat in. One man yelled out that there was another batch ready to be devoured as two others hoisted the container onto a dolly and took it over to the food tent, where festivalgoers eagerly awaited to purchase a meal and delight in the fact that this was truly fresh lobster.

Eugenia and Scott watched the lobstermen for a bit before heading over to the food tent. For $16, one could purchase a lobster dinner consisting of a whole Maine lobster with melted butter, an ear of corn, and a dinner roll. Other seafood items were sold á la carte. Eugenia and Scott both got a dinner, and some smoked mussels and shrimp to share since Eugenia had never had either dish cooked in that manner. They each got bottled water and a package containing a bib, a small fork to pick out the lobster meat from the claw, and a pair of hard plastic pliers to crack the claw.

After finding a table and putting on their bibs, Eugenia began to experience her first lobster dinner. Scott gave her a crash course on how to crack open the lobster, although Eugenia had picked crabs back in Maryland so she wasn't quite a novice. After getting the meat out of the claw, she tried it first without the butter. This was so much better and sweeter than crab meat she had eaten before. The meat was warm, sweet and delicious. She then dipped it in butter and was thrusted into heaven.

"Oh my God! This is so good!" she exclaimed.

Scott couldn't help but smile. "I know. Isn't it the best?" They continued to enjoy.

"Okay, you're going to think I'm crazy, but you know what this is reminding me of?" said Eugenia.

"What's that?" as he took a bite into his corn.

"Remember that scene from that movie Flashdance where Jennifer Beals is out on that date with Michael Nouri? So she's eating lobster and with one sexy move, she slowly tears it apart with her teeth. And Michael Nouri is going crazy because here's this pretty girl with bare shoulders, doing this seductive thing with her mouth."

"Eugenia, feel free to do that if you like," Scott coaxed her with a wicked smile on his face. "Don't let me stop you."

Eugenia just laughed, "Nah, that's okay. I just thought of that. Don't know why."

Scott showed her how to pull off the back shell of the lobster and Eugenia began picking the meat out of that section, noticing how much tougher it was compared to back fin crab meat. However, it was still enjoyable and had a bit of sweetness to it.

Scott stared at Eugenia and couldn't help but tell her, "You know, you have a beautiful smile, Eugenia. I like your dimples."

Eugenia actually blushed a bit, "Thank you. You too...you have a nice smile, too." *I can't believe I'm blushing,* thought Eugenia.

"Thanks."

"So tell me about this piano playing."

"Well, took lessons as a kid, played in the high school jazz band. As a teenager, I played mainly to get girls. Some of them seemed to like that sort of thing, some thought it was corny. I think it was more hip to play the guitar, but I always liked the piano. I stopped playing for a while in college then when I ended up here and bought this restaurant, the piano came with it. So I began playing again, practicing and playing for customers. It just kind of took. The singing, well, like I said, I must have been a lounge singer in my previous life. What about you, any musical training?"

"Well, I sang in my high school choir, sang alto. Now it's pretty much in the shower and in my car when I'm alone. Played the guitar a little bit. That's about it."

"Well, that sounds good. You can come and accompany me. I can see you now, in a red-sequin gown, standing beside the piano, and belting out a Pearl Bailey or Ella Fitzgerald classic while I play the piano in my tux."

"Oh, no. No way! Scott, where do you get these fantasies from?"

They both laughed. Eugenia shook her head and rolled her eyes.

Eugenia then tried the smoked mussels and shrimp and couldn't believe how delicious they were. They continued eating their meal and talking about how beautiful the area was.

"I was just curious—what was your last girlfriend like? You don't have to tell me, if you don't want to, but inquiring minds want to know." Eugenia said with a slight smirk on her face.

"Okay, I have a confession to make." *Okay, what's this about?* thought Eugenia. "I thought you were quite a bit younger, like 30."

"Really?"

"Yeah, but was happy to hear that you're 45. My last few relationships have been women, shall we say, of a certain age group, generally 10 to 15 to 18 years younger. And I found myself getting my heart broken a lot."

"Wow."

"Yeah. I guess with the hair, they think I'm younger. Then they find that I'm just an old windbag, doing corny things like wanting to have a conversation on the phone instead of texting, playing Frank Sinatra on the piano, not looking at Facebook every minute of the day. Often the conversations would go like 'I sent you a text. Didn't you read that?' Or, 'didn't you see the photo on Instagram? That's where I posted it.' And the movies they like, I had no interest in but went anyway. Once I fell asleep at the movies, had worked all day and was tired. That didn't go over very well."

"Wow. Where did you meet these very young ladies?"

"Well, at the restaurant or sometimes at parties. The last young lady that I dated was part of a bachelorette party. They came into the restaurant on their way to some bar. She was pretty, blond, very attractive. We started dating and probably dated for six months or so and it didn't work out. She was 29. I guess she thought I was rich because I owned the restaurant. Like I said, she found out I was this old windbag and that was that. My friends say that the women I date are too young for me. So, I must confess, I thought you were younger…."

"So that's why you asked me out?"

"Wait a minute, let me finish. Yes, you look younger than 45, but I was captivated by your beauty, was relieved that you were 45 and…and most importantly, you were related to Chuck."

Eugenia sat there staring at Scott for a minute and then smiled.

"Okay. You have redeemed yourself," Eugenia said quietly.

"Eugenia, that's the absolute truth." Scott stopped right there and took a sip of his water. *I'm tired of the games, the trying to be something that I'm not, the relationships going nowhere,* he thought, but stopped short of saying that.

Then Eugenia piped in, "Captivated by my beauty?" she repeated.

"Yeah, okay. That's a little dramatic, I know. But I think you're pretty and that's the bottom line."
Eugenia smiled. "Well, thank you."

"You're welcome. Are you finished?" he asked.

"Yes."

"Well, allow me to show you the rest of the festival."

After wiping their hands and dumping the trash, Scott and Eugenia stepped outside of the food tent and glanced out at the beautiful marina with the many boats docked in it. Couples, families with strollers, young people and older couples stood at the railing snapping selfies with the marina in the background.

Scott asked an elderly couple if they would take a couple of pictures with both Eugenia and Scott's cell phones and the gentleman obliged. Scott and Eugenia stood close together as Scott slipped his arm around Eugenia's shoulders. This was the closest she had been to him and she noticed how good he smelled, like a clean, soapy scent. She also was made aware of how much taller he was to her 5'7" frame. She estimated him to be around 6'2". Eugenia found herself edging closer to him, not feeling awkward at all, and for the second photo, she slipped her arm around his waist as well. For some reason, it felt like a good fit.

They both thanked the gentleman and then looked at the finished product. *Gosh, we look like a real couple,* Eugenia thought.

"Not bad, hey?" asked Scott. "No, not at all."

Scott grabbed Eugenia's hand and continued walking towards the other side of the festival grounds. They headed down a plank leading to a pick-up, drop-off point for one of the several commercial small boats that took visitors out into the bay where they could observe the boat operators catch lobsters. Scott told Eugenia there were several boats docked right near his restaurant that also took visitors out into Camden Bay.

"I'd be glad to take you sometime, if you want."

"That would be great," agreed Eugenia.

After seeing all that there was to see, Scott led Eugenia over to one of several benches overlooking the marina. They both sat and stared out into the bay. Scott sat comfortably with his ankle resting on his knee. As he explained that a naval ship comes to the harbor every year during Lobster Fest, he placed his arm on the bench behind Eugenia's shoulder. She once again caught that soapy fresh scent of Scott's. She brought up the subject of the earlier conversation about his preference for younger women and began to laugh. Scott said that maybe he was insecure or something, he didn't know. He then asked her about her last boyfriend, but gave her the option not to tell him if she didn't want to.

"Not much to tell. Seems like I kept running into guys who wanted to have more than one woman. I just wasn't having that. I was so wrapped up in my career, was always going to conferences, volunteering to go to different events that involved the marketing department, stuff like that. After my divorce, I worked on getting my Master's. Been pretty busy the last few years. I liked it that way."

Scott had changed positions, leaning forward, resting his elbows on his knees and turning slightly towards Eugenia as she spoke. She occasionally glanced at Scott as she spoke and noticed that he had taken off his glasses. He stared at her with the most beautiful brown eyes. Eugenia suddenly stopped talking, his eyes distracting her.

"What's wrong?" he asked. "You were saying that this bum, who, by the way, must have been out of his mind to fool around on you and let you go, that he wanted a harem or was a polygamist or something?"

"No, I hadn't seen you without your glasses. You have nice eyes."

"Thank you. So do you."

"Can I ask you something?" asked Eugenia.

"Anything!"

"Have you ever dated a black woman?"

"Yes, I've dated black women, Latino women, even a Muslim one. Why?"

"Just wanted to know."

"What about you? Black women? I mean white men. Okay, I said I'd keep the corny jokes to a minimum.   Although, nowadays that question isn't such a bad question. But I guess I shouldn't be asking it on the first date."

Eugenia just laughed. "Yes, I have dated white men before, but have never dated black women, nor Latino, white or Muslim women either, or any women for that matter. Does that answer your question?"

"Yes, not that it would be a bad thing if you had, just want to get that clear," said Scott, using his hands and being a bit animated. "Okay, let me pull my foot out of my mouth and cease with the corny jokes."

Eugenia continued to laugh. "You really have jokes, don't you?"

"Sometimes I wonder about myself and my jokes."
They sat quietly, watching the various boats come in and out of the harbor. Scott, once again, rested his arm on the bench behind her, then moved it onto her shoulder, moving over a little closer towards Eugenia.

"Are you having a good time, Eugenia?"

Turning to face him, she smiled and answered, "Yes, I am."

"Despite my jokes?"

"Despite your jokes," she assured him.

Dusk had settled over the harbor and they decided to head back to Camden. *I think I'll take her back to Fins. Hopefully she'll enjoy my surprise,* he thought. They then headed north on Rt. 1 as darkness fell on Maine.

"How about a night cap at Fins?" he asked.

"Sounds good."

As they entered the restaurant from the harbor side, Scott greeted the staff members warmly introduced them to Eugenia, who had caught the eye of Megan. When Scott had his back turned, Megan flashed Eugenia a thumbs up as she ducked into the dining room. Eugenia smiled. Leading Eugenia to the bar, Scott told her to order a drink and said he would be right back. There were two couples at the bar and each of them was engaged in a conversation. Eugenia ordered an orange crush and spoke to the bartender for a few minutes.

The piano sat a few feet from the bar but back in a corner. Where she sat, Eugenia would have to turn in order to see it. She then heard the now familiar sound. Scott had started playing a song called "Stairway to the Stars." Eugenia recognized it, recalling Henry Mancini made a version of the song, although there probably was a vocal version as well. It sounded beautiful and calming as Scott tickled the ivories. This was the type of song Scott said he liked to play—something from a bygone era, slow and melodic. He continued to play as Eugenia got up and wandered over to the piano. Looking up, Scott saw Eugenia by the piano, smiled, and gave her a sly wink. He continued to play, looking down at the keys and then back up at Eugenia. *I hope she's enjoying this. This is for her,* he thought. She continued to watch until he finished.

There was applause from the patrons and Eugenia clapped, also.

His next song was "Nice and Easy" by Frank Sinatra, and Scott began to sing. Eugenia remained standing, mesmerized by both his singing and piano playing. He had a good voice, could carry a tune, not Frank Sinatra mind you, but a good voice. She found herself swaying back and forth to the tune. It was another tune from a bygone era that Scott enjoyed playing. After he finished, more applause and even some shouts came from the patrons.

Scott motioned for Eugenia to come and sit beside him on the piano bench and she brought her drink over, placing it beside Scott's drink resting atop the piano. It was a beautiful baby grand piano, mahogany in color. He played once again slowly, a song called "A Thousand Years", this time not singing. Eugenia watched his long fingers touch the keys of the piano and the way they seemed to float over each and every note. She mouthed the words, singing silently to herself and listening to the melodic piano playing from this guy she just met. This was like no other date she'd ever been on. How could any woman think that this was corny? This was absolutely awesome! Eugenia continued to watch those long fingers effortlessly sail over the keys. He made it look easy although she knew that he had many years of practice. Occasionally Scott turned to smile at Eugenia before looking back at the keys. At the end of the song there was, once again, more applause and more shouts came from all over the restaurant.

Eugenia turned to Scott, "Wow. I am speechless, Scott." They continued to sit at the piano for a few minutes.

"Did you like that?"

"Oh my God, are you kidding, I loved it! Thank you so much."

"You're welcome. Did you recognize 'Stairway to the Stars'?"

"Yes, I did. Dad loved that song."

"He requested it every time he was here. He said your mother liked it."

"I didn't know that. Wow." Eugenia looked down, processing that information. Scott then put his arms around Eugenia's shoulder and held her for a few minutes. Eugenia then looked at Scott. "Thanks for playing that." He then kissed her on the forehead.

"Anytime."

Scott and Eugenia said their goodbyes and left the restaurant, climbing into the Scott's SUV and heading towards Eugenia's place. On the way home, as they traveled up Atlantic Avenue, Eugenia wondered if he would give her a good night kiss. How would that feel with his beard? *I guess it would tickle,* she thought, smiling to herself. She couldn't recall ever dating a guy with a beard. She also wrestled with the idea of inviting him in, not that anything would happen, but she still wrestled with the thought. She liked him, no doubt, and she was sexually attracted to him. But she knew that with past relationships, she had gotten intimately involved too quickly with guys, only later finding out that they didn't want what she wanted—a monogamous, committed relationship. *Yeah, we're taking this slow,* she thought, *nice and easy.*

The entire date had been pretty amazing and she did have a good time. Eugenia admitted to herself that she hadn't been "courted" like this... ever. With the flowers, opening the door, the piano playing, it was a bit overwhelming and would make the skeptical woman in her say—okay this is too much, this can't be real. But it seemed genuine and sincere. *Maybe I had to travel to Maine to find this*, she thought.

Should I give her a good night kiss? thought Scott. *Would that be too much? I'd love to, I really would. She does have a nice pair of lips. Maybe she'll invite me inside? I'd like that. Of course I had to play "Stairway to the Stars". What the hell was I thinking? But it's such a melodic, soothing song and I wanted to play it for her, for Chuck.*

Scott pulled up outside of the cottage, turned off the engine and looked over at Eugenia. "Well, I had a really great time," he said softly. "I hope that song wasn't too disturbing. Were you okay with it?"

She then looked over at him and nodded, "It was beautiful. Thanks again." *I guess I better be getting in here. I can't invite him in.* "Well, I'd better be going."

"I'll walk you to your door. Let me get that door for you." Scott hopped out of the car, went to the other side and opened her door.

"Thank you."

They then walked up the sidewalk and ascended the couple of steps onto the porch. She had left the porch light on so they'd be able to see where they were going. Eugenia fished her key out of her purse then looked up at Scott.

"What are you doing tomorrow?" asked Scott.

"Going back to the library and continuing my research. And you?"

"Well, I'm working during the day. My partners and I switch between days and evenings, although we do have managers there also. I'd like to take you to the Rockland Breakwater Lighthouse. Then we could go out to dinner at a place called The Lobster Shak that's in Rockland. How does that sound?"

"That sounds great! What time should I be ready?"

"How about 4?"

"Sounds good."

"The walk to the lighthouse is about a mile one way, so we'll be getting some exercise and it's along a rock wall. So sturdy shoes are in order. We'll get something to eat afterwards. So dress in shorts and comfortable shoes. Okay?"

"Okay. Looking forward to it."

They then stood there in the porch light and didn't say anything, looking into each other's eyes. Scott rubbed both of Eugenia's arms up and down.

"You have very soft skin," he whispered. *That felt good, those long fingers rubbing my arms,* thought Eugenia. *I don't want this evening to end.* Both of them shared feelings of awkwardness and desire, clumsiness and want.

"I'd better let you go inside." And with that, he pulled her closer, bent down and kissed her on the cheek. He couldn't resist and held her for a few minutes. *Can we stay like this forever?* he thought, mirroring Eugenia's feelings. She wrapped her arms around his waist and could smell that soapy scent that she smelled earlier. He smelled good. They stayed like this for a few minutes and then let go. Scott, once again, kissed her on her cheek, smiled and whispered, "See you at four tomorrow." Then descending the couple of steps, he walked down the side walk, waved goodbye, got into his SUV and drove off down the street. Eugenia watched as he turned the corner before going into her house.

Eugenia went into her bedroom and laid down on the bed, thinking about the entire evening. *This feels good,* she thought. *But I'm leaving in a week and a half. Gotta get back and start looking for a job.*

The kiss on the cheek was nice, Scott thought as he drove home. This is good!

She then heard the chime on her phone indicating that she had a text message. It was Scott and it read, *Had a great time and looking forward to tomorrow. Sweet dreams, hon. I thought I'd remind you of Maryland a little bit with "hon".* No doubt he was referencing the fact that so many Marylanders use this term of endearment. *How sweet.*

Good night to you, hon, she texted back. And with that, she got ready for bed and was soon asleep.

Chapter 9

Five Generations

As Eugenia opened the door to get her morning fix of exercise, a cool Maine breeze came rushing in. She locked the door behind her and stood briefly on the porch taking in the fresh air. She couldn't help but think that this felt like fall in Maryland. The air was crisp, cool, not at all like the end of July days she was used to.

Oh my God, I had a dream about Scott last night! What the heck was it about? she thought. *Oh yeah, I invited him in and we poured over the scrapbook and drank wine. He had his glasses off the whole time. Well, at least he had his clothes on. Whew!* She thought about how awkward it would be to see him later today if the dream was a little more risqué. *Whew!*

Eugenia decided to walk near Scott's house. She headed towards downtown, walking up the hill on Mechanic Street before making that left turn. She found his house and walked past it. Eugenia spotted his SUV out front, saw the motorcycle on the side—all was calm and quiet. *If he sees me, I hope he doesn't think I'm stalking him.* Continuing down to Rt. 1, she circled back through Main Street and headed home to get ready for another day of research. *Maybe I'll call Aunt Nell to see if she knows anymore.*

"Hey girl, how's it going?"

"It's going good, Aunt Nell. How's your ankle?"

"I'm coming along. You know how your Aunt Tess gets on my nerves. Can't believe we once lived under the same roof. How's that guy?"

Eugenia was surprised at the question and then remembered: *Oh yeah, Scott and I are on Facebook and so is Aunt Nell.*

"Good, real good."

"He's awfully cute, for a white boy. What's the story?"

She then told Aunt Nell about Fins and how they met. She told her about the piano playing and the Lobster Fest.

"Did you do that thing that Jennifer Beals did in Flashdance when she ate her lobster?" Aunt Nell asked with a laugh.

"No, of course not. But I did bring it up."

"I know you did. You're my niece, aren't you?"

"You are just bad, Aunt Nell," and they both laughed. They chatted a little more and then Eugenia asked if she knew anything about the Negro Island Lighthouse and her mom.

"What's Negro Island Lighthouse?"

"There're pictures of the lighthouse all around the cottage. Dad must have really liked that place. Negro Island Lighthouse is now Curtis Island Lighthouse. But back in the 1700s or 1800s, this white guy and his black cook came to the area and the cook made a comment that the island was his island. It was named Negro Island and a lighthouse was built which was then called Negro Island Lighthouse until about 1935. That's a long time for a landmark to have such a name and be named after someone who just claimed that the island was his, and it really wasn't."

Aunt Nell answered, "I don't know, although he did mention that Gayle had some connection to the area. That's about all I know."

"What about mom's side of the family? Is there anyone around that may know?"

"I don't know. You know your mom's parents are deceased and she was an only child. Hmm," Aunt Nell thought. "I'm afraid I don't know, sweetie. I'm so sorry. But if I think of anything, I'll let you know. I'll ask your other aunts as well."

"Okay. Well, I'll keep looking. Heading back to the library today to continue."

"Girl, you better get your head out of those books and go get that man."

"Don't worry, we're going out tonight. He's taking me to this lighthouse in Rockland, then out to dinner."

"Well, that's better. So he's pretty nice, huh."

"Yeah, brought me flowers, opens the door, sings to me."

"Wow, that's really nice. Have fun, girl. Sounds like old fashioned courtin'. That's pretty rare these days."

"Don't I know it! Well, if you can think of anything about the lighthouse mystery, let me know." There was a long pause at the other end before Aunt Nell piped in.

"You know, I kinda remember your dad mentioning something about Scott. It's coming back to me. You know, when you get old, that's the first thing that goes. Yeah, Scott, the piano playing man from D.C. I seem to recall him. I had never seen a picture of him, so when I saw him on Facebook, didn't recognize him. Can't remember specifics, but I recall good vibes."

"Wow, okay. Well, if you remember anything about *him*, let me know."

"I certainly will. Well, sweetie, you take care, you hear?"

"I will, you too. See ya," and they both hung up.

Eugenia took her place at the computer in the history section of the Camden Public Library once again, after greeting Jean and chatting for a few minutes. Jean was impressed by Eugenia's research skills and interest in the subject matter.

Eugenia opened her notebook and looked at the chart that she had drawn the day before to try to figure out where she was.

Eugenia Bailey (Anderson) great-great grandmother
↓
Samuel Pratt------------Margaret Anderson (Pratt) great-grandmother
↓
George Monroe---------------Eugenia Pratt (Monroe) grandmother
↓
Charles Watts----------------------Gayle Monroe (mother)
↓
Eugenia Watts

It served as a map and she could continue from there. If this information was true, she had discovered her two-times great grandmother. From the looks of things, she was going to assume that this was true and began researching Eugenia Bailey (Anderson). Eugenia turned to the scrapbook to look for more clues. She had already looked through the book before but now she knew more and wanted to review what she'd already seen, searching for clues. She then ran across pictures of her father and her mother, pictures of when she was a little girl, pictures of her father and his sisters and some pictures of people that she didn't recognize. And, as always, that was where she remained for the next few hours, lost in the pictures.

Eugenia found the photo of some unfamiliar women. It was an old photo, in black and white, carefully placed inside the plastic of the photo album. She carefully peeled the plastic back to look at the reverse side of the photo hoping that someone wrote something on the back. As she turned it over, low and behold, there was writing. The following was written— Five Generations— Gayle, age 1; Eugenia, age 20; Grandma Maggie, age 42; Grandma Eugenia, age 73; and Grandma Martha, age 98. As she stared at the photo, she wrote down her conclusion:

- Gayle was my mother
- Eugenia was my grandmother, Eugenia Pratt (Monroe)
- Grandma Maggie was Margaret Anderson (Pratt), my great grandmother
- Grandma Eugenia was Eugenia Bailey (Anderson), my two-times great grandmother
- Grandma Martha was Martha Freeman (Bailey), my three-times great grandmother.

The date on the picture read June 1950, because, back then, dates were printed on pictures when the film was developed.

My mother was about a year old. This is amazing how these names are matching those on the list. And whoever wrote this on here put the ages. How astonishing is this? So Martha was 98 years old? She then wrote down the approximate year that each woman was born, estimating 20 years between each generation.

- Martha Freeman (Bailey)—1852
- Eugenia Bailey (Anderson)—1877
- Margaret Anderson (Pratt)—1908
- Eugenia Pratt (Monroe)—1929-1930
- Gayle Monroe (Watts))—1949

She updated her chart by adding Martha Freeman (Bailey) and putting the approximate year that each ancestor was born.

Martha Freeman (Bailey) great-great-great grandmother — 1852
↓
Eugenia Bailey (Anderson) great-great grandmother —1877
↓
Samuel Pratt------Margaret Anderson (Pratt) great-grandmother —1908
↓
George Monroe---------Eugenia Pratt (Monroe) grandmother—1929-1930
↓
Charles Watts------------------------Gayle Monroe (mother) — 1949
↓
Eugenia Watts

Eugenia then showed Jean the photo and all that she had discovered; Jean was just amazed. Eugenia found herself fascinated by the images and knowledge of her mother's past. Five generations and an ancestor who lived to at least 98 years old! Anytime one delves into the past and uncovers ancestors, the knowledge just seems to bring about more questions. This is what Eugenia was feeling—who were these women? What were their lives like? And now she had uncovered an African American ancestor born in 1852, before the beginning of the Civil War. What was the status of this ancestor concerning slavery? Was she a free person of color or enslaved? Eugenia had these and other questions. She spoke to Jean about where to go next and Jean suggested that she research the last woman, Eugenia Potts (Freeman), listed on the original lists of names from the scrapbook.

Eugenia decided to pursue that tomorrow. She wanted to get home to get ready for her date that evening. She packed up her things and spoke with Jean for a few minutes.

"Do you mind if I do some research on my own?" asked Jean. "I'm curious as well. Someone left you such a treasure trove of information in that scrapbook. I'd like to see what I can find."

"Sure. I don't mind."

Chapter 10

Rockland Breakwater Lighthouse

Eugenia decided to wear a red and white paisley-print blouse that she tied at her waist, denim Capri pants, and tennis shoes with ankle socks. She wore her hair down, parted in the middle, cascading down to her shoulders and framing her face. She topped the look off with gold hoop earrings. Staring at herself in the mirror, Eugenia suddenly realized some resemblance to the women in the picture. Although the photo was in black and white, the women's skin tones ranged from light to what appeared to be dark mahogany. Her mother's complexion appeared to be similar to Eugenia's, a light copper color. As she looked in the mirror, she felt a renewed sense of pride being a descendant of such a beautiful group of African American women. She couldn't wait to tell Scott.

Eugenia found herself at the coffee table, looking at the picture when she heard Scott's knock on the door. Opening the door, she couldn't help but notice this tall, lanky, bearded white guy standing on her porch wearing jeans, a blue-green short sleeve V-neck t-shirt, tennis shoes and his slightly tussled dark brown hair with his neatly trimmed beard, dotted with strands of gray hair.

"Hey, wow you look great!" he exclaimed, greeting Eugenia.

"Thank you. How are you?"

"I couldn't be better."

"Come on in."

Scott took the same place on the couch, glancing over the paperwork spread out on the coffee table. He noticed the flowers that he had brought the day before still looking fresh in the vase on the fireplace mantel. Eugenia sat beside him on the couch, anxious to show him what she had found that day. She then showed him the picture and the writing on the back. Scott leaned forward fascinated by what she had found and was in awe of what she was saying. As Scott leaned in closer, listening and occasionally looking over at this beautiful woman beside him, Eugenia couldn't help but notice that fresh, soapy scent with which she had become familiar. For a moment, while telling him her discoveries, she was distracted by his scent, and amazed at how comfortable she felt talking to him. *This feels good,* she thought and continued her conversation.

This summer afternoon in Maine had brought about a slightly higher temperature than in the morning and the humidity had not increased since Eugenia's early morning walk. As they rode out of Camden headed south on Route 1, Eugenia reflected upon the weather forecast she heard for the Washington area earlier in the day—hazy, hot, and humid. Another day of "oppressive heat will plague the D.C. area" was the words that she recalled. *I am not missing that at all,* she thought.

"A penny for your thoughts?" Scott interrupted her train of thought, as he looked over at her as he drove down Route 1.

"I heard the weather forecast for D.C. earlier today. It was a typical summer forecast—hazy, hot and humid."

"I don't miss that a bit," Scott commented. "But the winters do get quite cold up here and we do have more snow. That's the trade off, I guess you can say."

Yeah, but maybe I'll keep better, was Eugenia's thought, referring to a line she had heard on some TV show, meaning the cold will help to preserve her, so to speak. *There goes that thought again, the notion of living here permanently. Well, I'd have to get a job, but expenses would be less since I won't have a mortgage. Only the taxes and, of course, the inheritance, the life insurance proceeds that dad left me.* The thoughts crept into her mind as she looked out the window at the bed and breakfasts that dotted the Route 1 landscape.

"Okay, I'm going to try this again, a penny for your thoughts," said Scott, making another attempt to pry into Eugenia's thoughts as they entered the town of Rockland.

Turning to Scott, Eugenia answered, "I'm sorry. Sorry I'm in such deep thought. I was just mulling over the possibility of staying here in Maine."

They had reached their destination. Scott pulled into a parking space, turned off the engine, and looked over at Eugenia.

"Really? I didn't think that was a possibility. I mean, wow. I think that would be great! I know we just met."

"Well, now, I'm just thinking about it. This place is so beautiful." She looked around at the trees and thought she saw a body of water in the distance.

"The expenses would be less, with the cottage and all. I'd have to find a job. The thought of going into another line of work, changing careers has crossed my mind. It's a big decision, after all," she said, looking over at Scott. She couldn't help notice those brown eyes behind his glasses as he sat there listening to her intently.

"It is a big decision," he reiterated. "It really is. But I see that you are hooked like I was on the beauty of this area. It's gorgeous, no doubt. People who come into my restaurant are usually tourists. People are in a good mood and we have very few gripes from customers. The chefs cook a great meal and then I put them in a better mood with my piano playing, not that I'm bragging." Eugenia couldn't help but laugh. "But it is nice here, a little more relaxing, slower pace, that's for sure. I think as I get older, I seek that slower pace."

"Yeah," Eugenia commented, as she looked out the window.

To reach the Rockland Breakwater Lighthouse, Eugenia and Scott walked through a wooded area along a dirt-covered path. There were other curious explorers; some were probably tourists, and some were locals who just wanted to enjoy the beauty of Maine. Once they got beyond the trees, Eugenia's eyes locked onto the body of water that she suspected existed, that she saw through the trees on shore. Before them was the Rockland Bay. Scott explained that the lighthouse sat at the end of a long, granite walkway. They both stood there for a few minutes, taking in the breathtaking beauty of the bay, the keeper's house, the lighthouse, the boats out in the bay and the green, tree-covered hills making up the horizon beyond the bay. What a sight!

"Are you ready?" asked Scott.

"Yes, by all means."

Scott then took her hand and led her down the dirt-covered path, leading to the granite walkway. Once they reached the stone path, Scott reminded Eugenia to be careful and to watch where she walked. Sometimes it was hard to hold hands on this path; one just had to negotiate the path on one's own. The granite could be slippery at times; although it had not rained that day, waves from the bay had splashed onto the rocks. There were gaps between the huge boulders and some of the stones set up higher than others, making what could be a challenging walk.

Eugenia and Scott were not alone as there were numerous explorers walking the path, some coming back, finishing the nearly two-mile round trip trek. There were other couples, a few families and some young people enjoying the solitude of the area. Several men stood on a lower level of rocks that ran parallel to the path with fishing gear, tossing their lines into the bay, hoping for the catch of the day.

Negotiating the rocks isn't too bad, Eugenia thought. *But I really have to watch what I'm doing and stop when I want to look out into the bay* or *anywhere else, for that matter. Can't walk and sightsee at the same time,* she thought. *No multi-tasking up in here!*

Scott stayed closely behind, occasionally stopping and letting Eugenia know about a boat or something interesting to look at. They both brought their phones and stopped occasionally to snap a picture. Scott took a picture of Eugenia with the lighthouse in the background. They took selfies and asked another explorer to snap a picture of them. *We look like a couple,* was Eugenia's thought as she examined the image. They continued on with Scott occasionally stopping to look at Eugenia ahead of him, noticing that she was doing just fine negotiating the rocks.

What a beauty, he thought. *What a beautiful woman.*

He had found himself recently trying to recollect what Chuck said about his only daughter. Scott remembered Chuck's words, "You would like Eugenia if you met her." Scott had no doubt about that—he liked Chuck and knew he was a good man. But, as Chuck said, she had her own life and no doubt, loves it back in Maryland.

I know we just met and I'm probably being too presumptuous, but I hope she finds a way to stay here.

After reaching the keeper's house and the lighthouse standing behind it, they explored the several levels of the structure, took some more pictures and headed on back, completing the almost two miles. As promised, Scott took Eugenia to The Lobster Shak, a restaurant in Rockland. Once again, they dined on a lobster that cost the unbelievable price of $20 and included two Maine lobsters. *This would have cost a fortune back in Maryland,* thought Eugenia.

The restaurant was definitely more of a summertime venue with outside seating only. A large canopy covered the picnic tables. Eugenia and Scott ordered the double lobster dinner that came with corn on the cob, a bag of chips and coleslaw. They each ordered a beer before sitting down to wait until their number was called.

"Wow, I can't believe this price!" exclaimed Eugenia.

"Got to be the best in town."

They sat for a few minutes in silence. Eugenia took in the scenery, looking over at the bay to her left and spotting several boats. There were quite a few patrons in the restaurant. *Must be a popular place,* thought Eugenia.

"So did you like the lighthouse?"

"Yes, very much so. Thanks for taking me," she said as she smiled at Scott.

"How was your day today? Sorry I didn't ask earlier. I was so wrapped up in my findings today. And because of certain granite walkway, I got distracted and really had to concentrate on walking."

Scott smiled. "Not a problem. Really good. We had a pretty busy lunch. Lots of tourist 'cause of the festival. Good time of the year. Oh, and Megan was asking about you. She told me to tell you hello the next time I saw you."

"Oh, that's so sweet. Very sweet girl. Did you play the piano today?"

"Yes, I did and she is a very sweet girl. One of my best waitresses."

"Not to change the subject, but I was wondering—can I ask you some questions? I was reading something or another recently and the article had some good dating questions in it. They're, what I guess you could call open-ended questions to ask on a date, when you're trying to get to know someone."

"You want to get to know me?" Scott asked, as he pressed his hand against his chest. "Really? Despite my corny jokes?"

"Yes, I would like to know a little more about you, if you don't mind."

"Of course, I don't mind the questions," he said seriously. "You can ask me anything."

"Okay. When is your birthday?"

"January 16th. And you know the year, 1970, since we were born in the same year."

Eugenia then answered, "Well, not exactly. I'm 45 right now but my birthday is September 12th. So I'll be 46 this year. So we're the same age now, but I'll be 46 later this year."

"Oh my goodness, I'm dating an older woman? You're a cougar?"

"Okay, well, yes I am." As they were laughing, they heard their number called. They headed up to the window to get their meals. After returning to the table, they put on their bibs and began eating their meals. Eugenia cracked open the first lobster, fiddled with the claw, dipped it in the drawn butter and savored the sweet taste of the meat. She thought again about the Flashdance scene but didn't bring it up. Scott brought up the fact the Eugenia was an "older" woman and they both laughed. They talked about the Rockland Breakwater Lighthouse and Scott mentioned that sometimes he walks out there by himself. He likes the solitude of the area, goes out there to think and enjoy its beauty.

Then he asked, "Where do you go to be by yourself and think about things?"

Eugenia thought about that for a while. "I really don't have any place that I can think of. I've been to Ocean City, Md., on conferences, and used to walk along the beach in the mornings. I've often thought that I should go back there on vacation, but never did. Besides walking along the beach, sometimes I'd grab a book and sit on the beach and read. There's something about the ocean, the sound of the waves that is very peaceful."

"Do you like to read?"

"I love to read."

"What was the last book that you read?" asked Scott as he removed his glasses and placed them on his head. *Okay, he has to stop distracting me like this,* she thought. *He looks so good without his glasses.* She then pulled it together and continued.

"Cane River," she answered. "It's by Lalita Tademy. She writes about her family in Louisiana, particularly the women. The book starts out after her grandmother dies, they find like $1,300 in her home under her mattress. And the story starts there—how did the money get there? It goes back to the times before the Civil War. Many of her ancestors were enslaved and it tells the story of how these women survived and persevered in the 18th and 19th centuries in the southern United States. The stories were often not pretty, but they survived the best they knew how." Scott was fascinated by Eugenia's explanation and the way she used her hands when she spoke of something about which she was passionate. And reading was obviously a passion.

"It's funny, but that sounds so much like the research that you are doing," commented Scott.

"I know, it's a funny coincidence, isn't it? What about you? Read any good books lately?"

"Nah. I can't say I have. I'm an online newspaper reader. I look at the Wall

Street Journal, sometimes the Washington Post to see what's going on back home, and read MSN. That's about it."

"Okay, another question from the article—what secret skill do you have?" Eugenia continued her questioning.

"Playing the piano used to be it, but everyone knows about that one." With some thought he continued, "Oh, I make the best steak on the grill."

"Really?"

"Not to brag, but yes. And if you like, I'd like to invite you over for a meal, sometime before you leave to go back home."

"Yes, that would be nice." Eugenia began thinking about what day that would be. She had planned to leave in about a week and a half. *Maybe I can stay longer,* she thought. *I'll have to think about this.*

"What about your secret skill?"

"I write."

"Really. What do you write? Poetry? Short stories? Novels?"

"Not poetry. Short stories mainly. I have quite a few on my computer. And I do keep a journal. I was the writer in my last job, writing pieces for the annual report, press releases. Everyone in my department hated to write— don't know why they were in the marketing department. So I got that job and it was the easiest part of my job. I guess it isn't a secret skill. But the short stories were something that I didn't tell anyone about. The salacious tales of sultry women, sexy men, passionate love stories, you know, stuff like that."

"You've peak my interest. When can I read them?"

"I'm kidding. They're not that sultry. Just stories. But I've been thinking since I started this research on my mother's family that I may record all of that history once I find out everything. Jean, the lady at the library, suggested that. She's been really helpful. She suggested that I keep everything in order and be sure to record the date that I find any facts about my family. Okay, ready for the next question?"

Before Scott could answer, Eugenia noticed quite a long line forming at the order window and stretching into the parking lot that ran parallel to Route 1.

"I think we'd better leave. They might want this table," stated Eugenia.

They cleared their table and headed to Scott's SUV, and soon were back on Route 1 headed north to Camden.

"Did you have any more questions?" asked Scott.

"Yes, I do."

Then he said jokingly, "Where did you want to continue the interrogation?"

"It's not an interrogation," Eugenia countered, laughing. "It's a means of getting to know you better and for you to know me better." She continued, "Don't you want to know me better?"

While stopped at a traffic light, Scott turned to Eugenia and said seriously, "Eugenia, more than you know." She just looked at him and realized just how serious he was. *Oh my*, she thought.

Scott returned his attention back to the road and continued down Route 1. "I have a proposal," Eugenia piped in, breaking the silence. "Can we go to your house and continue the 'interrogation'?" *Okay I didn't see that coming*, thought Scott. "Sure, that would be fine," answered Scott. *Hmmm*, Scott thought.

Eugenia's experience with philandering men took over her thought processes and the talk about getting to know one another brought to her mind the "bathroom check" that Sophia has always talked about. In one of their many conversations, Sophia said to check out the man's bathroom. Just casually go in to take a leak and while in there, go through the medicine cabinet, looking for any trace of a woman perhaps spending time there. Look for razors, makeup, extra toothbrushes already used, stuff like that. Women tend to leave something behind when in a relationship with a man. So Eugenia has put on her detective hat and will be doing some spying. *This isn't what you think, Scott. Well, maybe he's not thinking about 'that'. We'll see.*

They arrived at Scott's house in what seemed like record time. The sun had set over Maine and as they walked up the darkened walkway to his porch, the porch light, which had a motion detector, came on. Scott unlocked the door and ushered Eugenia in. She immediately heard the sound of music playing. Scott apparently left a radio playing and it played a smooth jazz station. Eugenia suddenly felt butterflies but played it off. *I'm a woman on a mission.* Scott flicked on a light switch and a lamp back in the right corner illuminated a room marked by gray, tan and black tones in the furnishings. The L-shaped couch first caught her eye with its charcoal-gray hue. A smoked gray coffee table sat in front of it. To the left was a loveseat with wooden armrests matched the same dark gray as the couch. A big screen TV anchored the room and the couch faced the TV, which hung on a back wall. There were built-in bookcases that contained several photographs.

Eugenia made her way over to the shelves to look at the pictures. Scott watched her every move after locking the front door.

"My parents, my sister, her kids. Me." Eugenia stared at the images and saw a resemblance between Scott and his sister, and Scott and his mom.

"I played basketball, as you can see."

"Cute shorts," said Eugenia. He had joined Eugenia and pointed out the picture of him sitting at a piano.

"That was some recital."

Scott turned off the radio, fired up his laptop and switched on Pandora radio. He tuned in a station that played piano tunes. "Would you like something to drink?"

"What do you have?"

"Beer, wine."

"I'll have some wine."

Scott disappeared into the kitchen through a door on the right of the TV. Eugenia was curious and followed him into the kitchen, peaking in as Scott reached into the refrigerator.

"Just being nosey."

"Come on in." She looked around once more. The kitchen had a tiled floor, light brown cabinets, stainless steel refrigerator, dishwasher and the typical appliances. The appliances, with the exception of the refrigerator, were black and contrasted with the light brown cabinets.

"Nice place," said Eugenia as she leaned against the counter watching Scott open the wine bottle.

"I had a designer work her magic. She was a friend of one of my partners. I'm glad you like it." He reached for the glasses in the cabinet and poured. He then walked over to Eugenia, gave her a half-filled glass, and toasted.

"Here's to me meeting you after knowing about you, to your dear father, to, what else. You know you could help me out here. I'm trying to remember everything, get this right, cause I'm a little nervous…"

Eugenia just smiled. "You're nervous?"

"A little. I have one of the most beautiful women that I've ever known in my kitchen and she just interrogated me." Eugenia felt herself blush. "I'm trying to say the right thing."

"Scott, don't be nervous. Why are you nervous?"

He then sighed, "I like you, that's all." He then took off his glasses and placed them on top of his head.

"To us, I hope." They then clicked the glasses and took a sip. Scott put his glass down, placed his hands on both of Eugenia's arms and rubbed them up and down. They then looked into each other's eyes as Eugenia put her glass down.

"Chuck talked about you and I've seen pictures of you on his phone, so really did know about you before I met you. It's kind of strange. I've always met the woman first then met the parents. So this is kind of reversed. But I'm glad I met you. Just as simple as that."

"I'm glad I met you too." They clicked their glasses once again and took a sip.

"Why don't we go back into the living room," said Scott as he grabbed Eugenia's hand and led her to the couch where they sat down beside each other. "I think we were in the middle of your questions."

"Oh, yes. The interrogation," she said with a smirk.

"What's your biggest pet peeve?" asked Eugenia.

"Wow. Let me think. I guess since I own a business, it's people who don't value their job. People who are constantly late for work and then unproductive when they get there. I try to hire people who are enthusiastic and want to get the job done. We hire many college students and we try to gauge their enthusiasm during the interview. Most of the people are not going to be with us long, but they still should value the fact that they have a job. When it comes to relationships, honesty is right up there. Just tell me the truth. Also, when a woman doesn't communicate a problem; she may think that it will go away. But it has to be addressed. So shutting down is one of my pet peeves. What about you, your pet peeve?"

"I guess negative people. I saw it in my last job and a couple of people at the job placement center. Some had been unemployed for a while, and I can't say that I don't blame them for feeling like they do, but it seemed every time someone said something positive, something that might work as far as getting a job, this person would just contradict it and say something negative. For instance, the counselors at the center suggested that volunteer work could be way to get a job. So while seeking a job, volunteering can be a good way to make contacts, spend days away from the computer and help someone in the interim. This one person piped in and said it is a waste of time, it doesn't lead anywhere, etc. Regarding relationships, honesty is right up there, also. I think I mentioned that in my last relationship, the guy wanted more than one woman but led me to believe that I was the only one. It was heartbreaking to say the least. Breaking a promise is near the top of my list as well."

Scott asked what kind of music she enjoyed. Neither of them seemed to have a preference; they both liked everything and agreed that music is so important. It can set a mood, make you feel relaxed, make you want to dance, bring back a memory, make you cry, put you to sleep, want to laugh at the lyrics, and even make you praise the Lord. Scott hoped that it made his customers want to eat and drink more. As they talked about their musical tastes, Michael Bublé's version of Sway came onto the radio. Scott got to his feet and asked Eugenia for this dance. After some protests, Eugenia got up and the next thing she knew, Scott had her swaying to the beat of the song. She quickly got in step with his cha-cha-cha and followed him as he led her across the living room. She found herself smiling and enjoying the dance. She knew the basic step of the cha-cha — one two cha-cha-cha, two two-cha-cha-cha — and found herself even putting her own steps in. It all came back to her of how her dad had taught her the steps. *This brings back memories,* thought Eugenia.

Afterwards, they sat back down, took a breath, sipped on the wine and talked about the concerts each had attended and where they saw a particular act. They spoke of some of the venues in the D.C. area and the acts they had seen there. Eugenia found herself sitting on the couch, shoes sitting in front of her on the floor, and one leg tucked under her as she sat on the plush couch. She laughed easily at some of Scott's stories of playing the piano at the restaurant. He sat beside her and turned to her, going through his experiences at Fins.

He gave her a tour of his home, showing her the three bedrooms and bathroom on the second floor. One was an exercise room with a treadmill and various sizes of weights spread out on the floor beside a weight bench. *So he does work out,* were Eugenia's thoughts. The second bedroom was his office and the third was the master bedroom with its king-size bed covered with a mauve-colored comforter, numerous pillows at the head of the bed, various pictures on the wall, a dresser, chest of drawers and a stand with a keyboard.

"Yes, I do practice on that," he stated.

Eugenia excused herself after mentioning to Scott that she had to use the restroom. Scott proceeded downstairs after showing her where it was located. *I'm here on a mission.* She went into the bathroom and, after taking care of business, she quietly opened the wooden medicine cabinet door and peeked in. All masculine items made up the contents—several male-type deodorants, a razor, scissors, male cologne, of which she took a sniff, various over-the-counter medicines, nothing narcotic, nothing alarming—the usual. On the shelves inside the shower-tub combination were a couple of bottles of liquid male-type soap. *Let me take a sniff of that. Hmmm. Smells like Scott! I guess that's enough for now. I'm satisfied.* And with that, Eugenia proceeded downstairs and joined Scott on the couch.

Before they knew it, it was around 11 p.m. and they were both yawning.

"I guess I better get you back home. I didn't realize how late it was. I've got to get up and go in around 10:30 a.m." Eugenia gathered up her purse, Scott got his keys and wallet, and took the short drive to Eugenia's cottage.

Turning off the engine, Scott faced Eugenia and said, "I had a great time. Thank you so much."

"Thank you. Thanks for showing me the lighthouse and dinner was great. You really dance very well. You know I learned the cha-cha from my dad. The steps just came back to me, like riding a bike I guess you could say. Good memories."

"I'm glad I could bring back a pleasant memory. Well, let me walk you to your door." Hopping out of his car, Scott opened her door and helped her out. The porch light illuminated the sidewalk as they climbed the porch stairs.

"I'll have to get one of those motion detector lights like you have on your porch. It could really save electricity."

"I could install it if you like?"

"Uh, yeah, I guess that would be okay."

"It'll be my pleasure."

Eugenia fished her key out of her purse, unlocked the door, placed her purse on the table just inside the door, and then turned back to Scott.

"Well, I guess I'd better get in here."

"What are you doing tomorrow?"

"Going back to the library to do more research. Jean said when I left today that she would see what she could find. She's so helpful."

"Are you doing anything tomorrow after you finish your research?"

"No, not really."

"Would you like to go back to the festival? They usually have some big name entertainment Friday night. I'd like to take you."

"Oh, yeah, I heard that group Tower of Power is playing. They're pretty good. Soul, funk group. Yes, that sounds great. What time should I be ready?"

"I guess 5 would be good. Does that work for you?"

"Great."

"Well, let me let you go." He then placed both of his hands on her arms, noticed that they were a little chilly. "Are you cold?" He then rubbed them up and down, warming them.

"A little."

"Eugenia. I have to confess, as I mentioned earlier, knowing your father, this is really strange. I'd like to kiss you," he said softly. "But…"

She then looked into his eyes, put her hand on his cheek and whispered, "Scott, I'm not going to break. I'm a grown woman and you just happen to have known my father."

"I feel like the kid who came to pick up his date, the father threatened him before they left on a date and now he's scared to touch his date. So he…" At that, Eugenia stood on her toes and kissed Scott on the cheek. As she pulled away, he put both of his hands on her cheeks and gently kissed her on her lips. He continued and pressed harder. Eugenia threw her arms around his neck, taking in his soapy scent and kissing him in return. They kissed for a few more seconds, Scott ending it with a few light kisses on her cheek and Eugenia could feel the scratchiness of his beard. As they pulled away, Eugenia still had her arms around his neck. He held her and pulled her into his arms.

"That was nice, babe," he said and they stayed like that for a few seconds, then he let go.

"Let me let you go," he said softly. "Good night, babe."

"Good night," And with that, she stood in her open door and watched him go to his car, then waved good-bye and shut her door.
Okay. Wow. He's a really good kisser, she thought as she leaned against the door. She then collected thoughts together and proceeded to the bedroom to get ready for bed. *Wow, he's so charming. Okay, I did the bathroom thing. Looks good. He keeps asking me out. That's a good thing. God, he's so sexy!*

She then thought about the fact that she was leaving in a few days. *Can I really stay here?* As time went on, she thought about this and the possibility became more and more real. *I like it here,* she thought. *I really do.* The beauty of the town and its quiet, slower pace was getting more and more appealing.

Settling into her bed, Eugenia thought about Scott's arms around her, embracing her, holding her. His scent, his long piano fingers warming up her arms tonight. She couldn't help but smile as she sank into a deep sleep.

Chapter 11

Ezekiel Benjamin Freeman

E ugenia woke at around three in the morning to go to the restroom. She found herself thinking about Scott and the date from the last evening. She felt so good about this relationship, even though it had only been a short time. *I guess at 45, I know what I want and how I feel about things. It's nice being this age. Nothing like the way I felt about Ray,* she thought, referring to her ex-husband. *We were so young,* she thought lying on her back in bed. *He was so cute, though.* She finally drifted back to sleep.

At a little after nine, Eugenia made her way into the Camden Public Library, feeling more at home every day, saying good morning to the now-familiar faces of staff members. On her way to the first floor history section, she stopped by the glass display case that had the story of Negro Island Lighthouse, staring once again at the captions and the pictures before proceeding up the stairs into the history room.

Jean greeted her with such a grin that Eugenia became a little suspicious. Jean had been very subdued up until now.

"Oh my goodness, Eugenia, you're not going to believe what I found?" as she practically pushed Eugenia over to her computer and into the chair. Jean then put her half-wit eyeglasses on and brought up the sleeping computer screen to show her what she had found. Jean found the website of the Rockland Public Library located in nearby Rockland that also had a history section containing more information than Camden's library, since Rockland is the county seat of Knox County, Maine. Often the library in the county seat has more of an extensive repository of historical information. "I found this information," said Jean, showing Eugenia an index of the records that were stored at the library. It included a brief summary of what is there although one has to go to the library to do the research in order to seek out the contents of the information. This data is not online.

"Look at this. I found a record of a man by the name of Ezekiel Benjamin Freeman and his connection to the Negro Island Lighthouse. Ezekiel had a wife by the name of Eugenia."

Eugenia just stared at this as chills ran up and down her spine. "What does this mean, Jean?"

"Well, on the library's website is just a listing or index of the records that are stored there. You have to travel there to look at what they have. It may be writings on microfilm or in book form. You have to go and see. Sometimes individuals donate to libraries histories of their families, family trees, all kinds of information. You'd be surprised."

"Oh, my goodness, Jean! What a find! I saw the library when we went over there the other night to the Lobster Fest. I remember the building."

"We?"

"Oh, yeah, I met this guy, he plays the piano at Fins. He's the owner. He took me to the Lobster Fest the other night."

"Oh, yeah, Scott. Nice. I know him. Cute," she said with a grin.

"Yes, yes he is," Eugenia said smiling. "Well, better be going."

"I figured you would. Just see Pat. She'll be expecting you. Been meaning to ask you—I know you said that you were leaving, just staying here two weeks. Are you still going?"

"Well, Jean, the thought has been on my mind."

"The reason I ask, I know you said you were looking for a job. I remember you telling me. Well, there is possible position opening over at the Rockland Library. Not sure if it is in the history department or the regular library. Don't know how much they pay. But here's the website," and she wrote it down. "Go online and take a look, if you want. I know this isn't like D.C., but it's nice here, it really is. And with your marketing background, well, you never know where things might lead."

Eugenia stared at the computer for a few more minutes looking at that name—Ezekiel Benjamin Freeman, wife Eugenia, a possible job opening up. Her mind was spinning. She then gathered her things and said good-bye to Jean.

"Thank you so much."

"You're more than welcome, dear. Let me know what you find."

Eugenia got on Route 1 and tried not to speed going through Rockport. She finally made it to Rockland, parked her SUV, and practically ran into the library. The 18th century building was a step back in time, beautiful light-colored brick and wooden doors. This stately structure looked like a library.

She quickly found Pat who ushered her into the history part of the library. Jean had told Pat that Eugenia was coming and Pat had pulled out several books, some paperwork and other materials for Eugenia to peruse. Eugenia got to reading.

Remembering her high school history classes, Eugenia recalled reading thick textbooks where much research was done about American history, the Civil War, and the American presidents. But history books exist that contained local history. Local historians gather information about the story of local people as well. And that's what she delved into today.

She read over the history of Camden once again and the story about Negro Island. Still fascinating. Then she found a little more about James Davis, the man who came with his wife to Camden, Maine.

> *Captain James Davis came to Camden in approximately 1827 with his then-pregnant wife. Their African cook, Ezekiel, accompanied them. Ezekiel was reported to be about 15 years of age. As they approached an island out in Camden Bay, Ezekiel shouted that this was his island, no doubt captured by the beauty of the five-acre plot of land. At some point it was named Negro Island. The threesome remained in Camden for a few years. Mary, Captain Davis' wife, had lost the child while giving birth. The three of them eventually settled in Washington, D.C., leaving the beautiful area behind.*

> *Mary died in 1831. Ezekiel remained Captain Davis' cook until Davis' death in 1838. According to James Davis' will, Ezekiel was to be freed at the death of Davis. Ezekiel continued to live in D.C. He then took the name of Ezekiel Benjamin Freeman, no doubt proud of the fact that he was indeed a free man of color. He married Eugenia Potts in 1840.*

Oh my God! Eugenia stopped reading and rummaged through her paperwork to find the listing of the women. There it was: Eugenia Potts was the last woman listed, most likely her four-time great grandmother. She sat back for a few minutes and then continued reading.

> *Ezekiel Benjamin Freeman joined the United States Colored Troops (USCT) in 1863 and was part of the Union Army during the Civil War.*

Along with fighting for the freedom of his African American brothers and sisters, he was hoping to travel back to Maine to see "his" island. James Davis made sure that Ezekiel was literate and Ezekiel was an avid reader. He read that the island was now called Negro Island and he wanted to return. Unfortunately, he would never return. He served in the Civil War, witnessed the emancipation of his enslaved brothers and sisters, remained in Washington D.C., and lived the rest of his days in the capital city.

The narrative ended there so Eugenia sought Pat to show her what she had found and ask for advice. Pat explained how she could find the Freemans in the 1850 and 1860 U.S. Census records. Eugenia continued her search, looking through the hand-written, cursive writing of both censuses. Again, she printed blank census forms and hand-wrote the information that she found, making sure to document everything that was there.

The hours seemed to fly by. Eugenia found herself looking at the information contained in the census records. Rubbing her eyes that were no doubt affected by the cursive writings of the census enumerators, Eugenia was both encouraged and fascinated.

After much searching, she found what she was looking for in the 1860 census. The census read: Ezekiel B. Freeman, age 48, Eugenia Freeman, age 40. Ezekiel's race was listed as Black and Eugenia's was Mulatto. Ezekiel was a cook and Eugenia didn't have an occupation listed. The children included a daughter by the name of Martha (even though the 1860 census does not list the relationship of persons in the household to the head of the household, most likely children listed under the first person are the offspring).

- Eugenia Potts (Freeman)
- Martha Freeman (Bailey)
- Eugenia Bailey (Anderson)
- Margaret Anderson (Pratt)
- Eugenia Pratt (Monroe)
- Gayle Monroe (Watts)

Eugenia referred to the list of women once again and found *Martha Freeman* (Bailey). Martha was 98 years old in the photo that had the five generations of women in her family. Sitting back, Eugenia looked at the photo, the census and found herself studying it all. She couldn't believe what she had discovered and found herself with a mixture of emotions: she felt pride, accomplishment, and empowerment. Tears formed in her eyes as she looked at the photo once again. She is descended from free people of color. She is descended from slaves, a Civil War veteran. She is descended from a beautiful group of women who lived long, full lives. She has ties to Camden, Maine. She is descended from a man who claimed an island but never was able to return. She walks the same soil as he. Eugenia reflected on how her mom had died so young of breast cancer and was not able to live such a long life. That made her sad, but she was able to learn something about her mother—something that her mother probably left her—something of which she was proud.

Eugenia wiped her eyes and began to transcribe the contents of the census records onto the blank census form, every so often pausing to reflect upon what she had found. She made copies of the narrative and made sure she wrote down the date, where it was from and other pertinent information. She just couldn't believe her discovery.

The hours had flown by and she decided to wrap it up for the day. Before she left, she went over to speak to Pat.

"Oh, my goodness, that is so great. What an incredible story!" Pat exclaimed as Eugenia hugged her.

"I know. Thank you so much!"

Packing up everything, Eugenia climbed into her SUV and headed north back to Camden. She couldn't wait to tell Scott. Once she got home, she spread out everything onto the coffee table.

The weather had gotten slightly hotter and Eugenia found herself sweating. She jumped into the shower. Afterwards she put on some lotion, fixed her hair, parting it on the side and letting it cascade down to her shoulders. Slipping into a sundress and putting on her gold hoop earrings, necklace, sandals, Eugenia settled on the couch to look over the information that she had gathered. There was a knock on the door and Eugenia saw Scott through the peep hole. He had gotten a haircut. It was more like a trim, just slightly shorter than it was, but still relatively long.

Opening the door, Eugenia exclaimed, "Hello. I like your haircut!"

Scott then took his hand and pushed back a few errant strands of hair that had landed on his forehead. "You like it?"

"Yes. Very nice," Eugenia complimented.

"Good. My goodness. You look great!" he said, bending down to kiss her on the cheek. Scott wore a navy blue tank top and a pair of plaid shorts that came past his knees and sandals. Eugenia noticed the now-familiar soapy scent as he kissed her.

"Come on in." Scott took a seat on the couch at the coffee table, looking over the vast array of newspaper articles, hand-written census forms, and the photo. Eugenia bubbled over as she told him about the information that she found. She stood in front of him, moving around the table, excitedly showing him the various pieces of paper. After showing him the photo of the five generations, Scott commented on how he could see the resemblances between the women and Eugenia. She showed him the census records, narrative and all that she had collected. Eugenia was like a bee, circling a nest, the way she went from one end of the table to the other. She must have been speaking to him a hundred miles per hour. He was listening intently, fascinated and captivated by her excitement, and watching her arms wave when she described something, noticing the inflections in her voice. Occasionally she bent down and he couldn't help but notice a little cleavage. He noticed how her light copper colored complexion had gotten slightly darker since he had met her due to the time that she had spent in the sun since her arrival. This is the first time that he had seen her in a dress. The dress' length came slightly below the knees and, although he had seen her in shorts, the dress was an improvement, showing different curves.

"You're going to write this up, right? I mean, this could easily be a book. There isn't much African American history in this part of Maine," he said looking up at her.

Suddenly Eugenia stopped in her tracks standing and just stared at Scott. She was going to put it together but for her own personal use.

"I could. I really could," as if a light bulb went off in her head. "This is just the tip of the iceberg. There's so much more research to do. What a great idea. Thanks so much." Eugenia then sat next to Scott on the couch, wrapped her arms around his neck and kissed him on the cheek. She then hugged him. Scott held onto her tightly.

"You're welcome." He continued to hold her for a few minutes and then pulled away, kissing her briefly on the lips. "I'm going to come up with more bright ideas if I get a thank you like that." They both laughed.

"Well, I guess we'd better head to the fest."

Scott got to his feet, pulled her up and hugged her again.

"Let's go," Scott said, turning away in order to hide his somber expression. *She'll be leaving in about a week*, he thought. Grabbing his keys that he left on the table beside the door, he waited for Eugenia to grab her purse and they headed to Rockland. Eugenia continued to babble on about her findings. Scott listened but said little, the thought of her leaving stayed in his mind. He decided that they would need to spend as much time as they could before she left.

It's a big decision. I know it was huge when I came here. We just met and I couldn't ask her to stay. But she's so beautiful, smart, reminds me so much of my friend Chuck. What a great daughter he brought up.

They found a place to park and made the three to four blocks walk to the Maine Lobster Festival. They again dined on lobster under the big tent by Rockland Harbor. Eugenia asked Scott about his day and he told her about his day at Fins.

"Are you okay?" asked Eugenia. She noticed that he was a little quieter than usual.

"Yeah, I'm fine. Rough day," he lied, looking away at the harbor and then looking down at his food.

"Scott," she said seriously and, as he finally looked up at her, then continued, "Jean from the Camden Library told me about a possible job opportunity at the Rockland Library. I went online and applied."

With the most serious look Eugenia had ever seen, Scott replied, "Eugenia, you're kidding me, right? Don't joke about that, please."

"Scott, I'm very serious. The position is in the history department. Oh, my God, I'm so excited." Eugenia seemed to light up when telling him about this news. "I'd be helping library patrons with research. I would also help schools out, all kinds of interesting stuff."

"Oh, my God, I can't believe it. You want to stay?"

"Yes, I would but I haven't gotten the job yet. I haven't even been interviewed. I have my severance and insurance proceeds from my dad. So even if I don't get it, I'll be okay financially, *for a while*. I can't promise that I'd be able to stay. I have to work and earn a living, you know. But I've been thinking about it since I set foot in this town."

Scott got up, walked to the other side of the table, and sat next to Eugenia. Putting his arm around her and, with both of them dressed in lobster bibs, he planted a kiss on her lips in front of few hundred people who sat amongst them under the tent. *Okay, he tastes like lobster*, Eugenia thought. But that's okay. He kissed her for a few more minutes. He then pulled away.

"But what if you don't get it?"

"Like I said, I can't promise I can stay. I've got to work."

"Of course. I understand."

"There are so many things to consider: putting my condo on the market, for one. It's a big decision."

"I know. But I'm glad you applied for the job. Hopefully you'll get it and can stay. I know we've just met. I have no right to ask you to stay. But I truly hope that you can." Eugenia looked at him, sighed and took a sip of water, not saying anything. Scott got up and moved back to the opposite side of the picnic table. Eugenia took a sip from her bottled water and continued to eat her dinner.

"I know one thing — I could get used to this lobster, especially at these prices." They both laughed.

As they ate their dinners, Scott and Eugenia chatted more about logistics of what was needed to relocate. Scott wanted so badly to ask her to stay. She could move in with me, *I've got plenty of room*, he thought. But he didn't dare ask. They finished their dinner and began to walk around the festival grounds, hand in hand.

"Well, if worst comes to worst, you could always move in with me. I have plenty of room. I mean, I know you have expenses with the cottage, taxes and all. You could become a kept woman."

Eugenia stopped in her tracks, let go of his hand and gave Scott the dirtiest look. *I don't believe he said that. No, he didn't!*

"Oh, my God, I don't believe I said that. Should I try to pull my foot out of my mouth? Look, it was another corny joke. You know I'm kidding, right?"

She then crossed her arms and said, "You better be." She wasn't as angry as he thought she was. She wanted to make him squirm a bit before she let him off the hook. "Really, Scott?"

"Eugenia, I'm sorry. I was joking. I swear." And at that, Eugenia burst out laughing. Scott stared at her and then laughed himself. "Kept woman? Where did you get that term?" and they both laughed.

But, for some reason, that comment made her think about the women in the photo and what their lives could have been like as black women in the early 19th and 20th centuries in America. She was beginning to form ideas of what she could write. She thought about the women in Cane River and what they did to survive in Louisiana in the 1800 and 1900s, which by today's standards would shock and disgust some people. But it was a different time, where the views, laws, customs for women were quite different.

Scott and Eugenia headed over to the stage and found seats for the Tower of Power concert. Scott was so glad that she wasn't mad at him; that look she gave him earlier really threw him for a loop.

Scott and Eugenia watched as the band set up. Finally, they began to play. Occasionally, since they were sitting in seats on the end and there was space in an aisle next to them, Scott would get up and ask Eugenia to dance. The band sang a couple of songs with a slower tempo and Eugenia found herself in Scott's arms, pressed against his body and swaying to the beat. He would occasionally spin her around and she was quickly back in his arms, taking in that soapy, fresh scent that he exuded. *Wow,* was her thought.

Chapter 12

The Sleepover

W ould you like to stop by Fins for a nightcap?" Scott asked as they traveled in his SUV north to Camden following the concert.

"Sure."

They arrived at Fins and Eugenia took a seat at the bar, enjoying her orange crush that she had ordered. Scott went into the back and let Eugenia know that he would only be a few minutes. She chatted briefly with the bartender and spotted Megan as she came over to chat with her. After a few minutes, Eugenia heard the sound of the piano and moved to sit a little closer. He then began to play "That's All" and Eugenia remembered a version by Nat King Cole but also recalled a more recent version by Michael Bublé. Scott then began to sing and Eugenia listened to the words. *He really has a nice voice.*

The song tells of a man singing to his love revealing to her that he is of limited means. He can only give her the simple things in life and there are others who can give her substantially more. But he is promising her the love he has and he is simply asking for her love in return.

After Scott finished, the sound of applause rang out. Scott signaled Eugenia to join him on the piano bench. Scott continued to play and began his rendition of "Stairway to the Stars". Eugenia sat there mesmerized by this man's piano playing. His long fingers literally "tickled the ivories". It was both soothing and relaxing, reminding her of a by-gone era. *Beautiful.* And, of course, this was one of her father's favorites and she listened intently. Once again, the sound of the audience's approval rang out at the end. Scott wrapped his arm around Eugenia's shoulder and gave her a quick hug. Eugenia remained by his side on the bench as he played a few more tunes for his audience and even took a couple of requests. Some of the tunes were a little more upbeat. Afterwards, some of the restaurant patrons came over and chatted with Scott, complimenting him on his piano playing.

To her surprise, Eugenia looked up and saw Jean from the Camden Public Library approaching the piano and Eugenia rose to greet her.

"Oh, my goodness, how are you?" Eugenia said, surprised at her presence. They exchanged hugs and Jean introduced Eugenia to her husband.

"Want you to meet my husband, Edward. Edward, this is Eugenia, the young lady I mentioned who's been coming into the library researching her family."

They shook hands. "So happy to meet you," said Eugenia.

"I've heard a lot about you. Very nice to meet you, too."

Eugenia turned around and as Scott rose, breaking away from some of his "fans", he acknowledged Jean and said hello to Edward. *I guess they know each other,* thought Eugenia. *Oh yeah, I remember her saying how cute he was.*

"Nice to see you both again. It's been a little while."

"Eugenia reminded me of your piano playing the other day, so I thought we'd come by, get a bite to eat and was hoping we'd catch a show. I guess we showed up on a good night," said Jean.

"So you've been helping my good friend here with her research. It's amazing what she's found," said Scott, looking over at Eugenia with an obvious sense of pride in his voice and a smile to match. He was in awe as to what she had found and it showed. *He called me his good friend,* thought Eugenia.

Eugenia explained to Jean where her research had taken her, acknowledging the information that she had found at the Rockland Library with the help of Pat. Scott, Edward and Jean listened intently as Eugenia told the story of Negro Island.

"I'm so glad that you went there. I knew there was more information. Good for you! How exciting!" said Jean.

"And I applied for the position over there."

"Oh, my goodness! That's great! Good luck. I'll put in a good word for you," Jean said as she grabbed Eugenia's hand and gave her an encouraging squeeze.

"Thank you so much." Eugenia was grateful for the acknowledgement and enthusiastically told her about the job's tasks. One of the things taught to her by the job counselors at the assistance center was to sound enthusiastic and eager about a potential opportunity. But Eugenia didn't have to pretend—she was passionate about this opportunity and it was obvious in her voice and her demeanor.

The four chatted more for a few minutes. Other restaurant patrons occasionally dropped by the group and complimented Scott. He introduced Eugenia to the people that he knew, but most were from out of town, so he wasn't familiar with them. Every time he introduced Eugenia to a familiar face, he acknowledged her as his good friend. *I can accept that*, she thought.

At Eugenia's suggestion, they went to Scott's place after leaving Fins. Scott was a little surprised but took her up on the offer. Eugenia was feeling somewhat more relaxed with him, had done the "chick check", and concluded that he probably wasn't seeing anyone else, although the jury was still out. It's only been a few dates.

She liked his place. She has to do some improvements to hers, she knows, maybe get rid of the outdated furniture and update a couple of things. *Dad was pretty miserly with his money, so replacing that furniture was probably a thought that never entered his mind.*

Eugenia took her "place" on the plush L-shaped couch and found herself, again, taking her shoes off and feeling at ease. Scott brought back a couple of glasses of wine. *Wow, she looks comfortable*, he thought. *I'm glad.*

"So, what was your first wife like?" Eugenia began the conversation. She had decided she needed some more information.

At first, Scott was taken aback by the question, but then he dove on into the subject matter. "Wow...Uh, okay. Well, Barbara was beautiful, smart, and quite shy when we first met. We met in college and she was from a good Catholic family from Montgomery County."

"Like me, from Montgomery County and Catholic."

"You're Catholic?"

"Yes, I am."

"So am I."

"I've been meaning to ask about a church in the area. Wanted to attend Mass on Sunday," inquired Eugenia.

"Yes, Our Lady of Good Hope. Don't know the Mass schedule. I'm afraid I'm not much of a practicing Catholic."

"Well, I can go online and get that information. Go on, you were telling me about Barbara."

"Oh, yeah. Kind of quiet, shy. We met at a party in college. We began dating and the next thing I knew, she was pregnant. She knew nothing about birth control and neither did I, for that matter. I was this stupid irresponsible college student. So we got married. She was in her junior year and dropped out; I was a senior and we decided that I would finish. She eventually finished, though. We struggled for a long time after getting married, raising Chloe. I was in the delivery room and the minute I saw my daughter, I knew she was the light of my life." Scott's face just lit up.

"We stayed married until Chloe was 15 and Barbara couldn't take my philandering any more. We divorced but it should have been long before that."

"You messed around on her?"

He looked directly at Eugenia and answered, "Yes, I did. I'm not proud of it at all. We were not compatible; she kept so many things inside of her. And when it did come out, it had boiled over and came out as an explosion. Sometimes I just couldn't stand it. When I think of it, we wasted so many years of our lives by staying together. But we agreed on one thing—we wanted Chloe to have a two-parent, stable home. We thought it was best."

"Did Chloe ever see your arguments or disagreements?" inquired Eugenia. Scott put his head down, as if trying to recall.

"No, no, I don't think so. We never argued in front of her, that's for sure. But we had many late night shouting matches. So, hopefully, she was asleep."

"Did you ever hit her?" Eugenia was just curious and a little surprised at the fact that she asked. But she knew she needed to know.

"Oh, no. No, it never came to that. But it got bad sometimes and, I must admit, felt like it. I would leave at those points." He then looked up. "I found out that she had messed around and that was pretty much the end. It's really weird—I think men can mess around and kind of expect the woman to deal with it. But men cannot deal with their woman messing around on them. That was the last straw. Although, thinking back, I couldn't blame her. I was such a dick back then. Like I said, smart woman, really too good for me. The divorce was the best thing that happened. We get along fine; we always did agree on what was best for Chloe. Like I said, she's got her mother's brains; she's going to be okay," he said with a nod and a look of pride on his face.

He then looked up at Eugenia. She had adjusted herself where she had tucked one leg under herself and looked completely relaxed. Scott got up, went into the kitchen, and grabbed the bottle of wine from the refrigerator. He poured Eugenia another glass, at which time she didn't stop him.

"So, since we're talking about exes, may I ask you about your ex-husband? I mean, if you want to talk about him."

"Sure. Well, met Ray in college. He actually didn't finish. He dropped out in his junior year. Ray was from this family in Potomac, one of the few black families who lived there."

"Potomac—wow, that's money!"

"Yeah. A bit of a spoiled brat, if you ask me. But he was a charmer and fine. Whew, so fine." Scott laughed. "As I recall, his father owned some hugely successful business—don't remember what and his mother was in charge of some non-profit. Anyway, they coaxed him into going to college and he stayed there for quite a while. We met while members of the Black Student Union and we hit it off. We dated for a couple of years. He dropped out but we still saw each other, against Daddy's wishes."

"I bet Chuck was thrilled about that?"

"Oh, you know he wasn't. He knew who Ray's father was. Ray's father was a Black Business Man of the Year, earned all kinds of awards. And his son, who pissed off his years at college and then dropped out, dating his daughter? Yeah, he wasn't thrilled at all. I think he was scared that I'd do the same thing. But I was determined to finish and I did. I had my head wrapped on pretty tight.

"So we eloped, against my family's wishes. It was pretty good that first year. Ray worked for his dad starting off in the mailroom. His dad wouldn't have it any other way. I had started working at the bank and, needless to say, was making more money than he. He wasn't crazy about that. Then the infidelity started. The next thing I knew, he had a daughter. So that was it. He had charmed the pants off of someone else." Eugenia took a sip.

"We divorced and he went on his merry way. I went back to school to earn my Master's. Dad was a bit disappointed in me for marrying Ray. So, during those years, we didn't see each other much. I think that's when he had begun coming up here. But over the years, we communicated with each other more and more and, finally, made up. That's pretty much about it. All the gory details."

"I don't think divorces are fun any way you look at it."

The wine was making Eugenia tired in addition to feeling mentally exhausted by that explanation of Ray. She laid her head down on the couch as Scott went into the kitchen in search of some cheese to go with the wine. After rummaging around in the refrigerator and finding some Asiago and sharp cheeses, slicing the blocks, putting them on a platter, he returned to the living room only to find Eugenia asleep. She had curled up on the couch in a fetal position and was sleeping peacefully. He set the plate down and sat beside her on the couch. She didn't move. He watched her for a few minutes to see if she would awaken. No such luck.

He went upstairs to his bedroom, retrieved a comforter and pillow from his bed, returned to the living room, and spread it over her. He gently lifted her head and placed the pillow under it. He tucked the comforter under her; she still had not awakened. He stood there for a few minutes watching her sleep before bending down and gently kissing her on her cheek. "I love you, Eugenia," he whispered and kissed her once again, moving a stray piece of hair out of her face. He then turned off the radio, turned out the lights, returned the tray of cheese to the refrigerator and, leaving a nightlight on, retired to his bedroom. He removed all his clothes, changed into only his pajama bottoms, laid in his bed, and felt a slight breeze come through the opened window.

In the darkened room, he laid there thinking. He couldn't get to sleep right away, knowing this beautiful woman was laying downstairs on his couch. *Maybe she'll wake during the night, come up and lay down beside me,* he thought. *I could then tell her how much I've grown to love her to her face, and not the chicken-shit thing that I just did. I could hold her in my arms all night. We could make love.* He couldn't believe how much he loved her in such a short period of time. He laid there for a few more minutes before finally drifting off to sleep.

Oh, my God, what have I done? Eugenia thought as she peeked over the burgundy comforter that kept her warm. She looked around and was acutely aware of all of her senses, as each one came alive in this strange environment. She noticed a nightlight in the corner and a light from the street lamp shown through the front window as well. She could smell Scott on the comforter, soapy smell and all. The comforter was soft to the touch. A slight scent of the opened bottle of wine hit her nose and she could taste the remnants of the wine in her mouth. *I guess we killed that bottle.* It stood on the nearby coffee table, not a drop left, only the residue. Occasionally a car passed by and she could hear the roar of an engine as it pierced the silence of this quiet town. There was no other sound.

I fell asleep on my date. Geez, I guess between the explanation about Ray and all this drinking that I was doing, it knocked me out!

Pulling off the comforter, Eugenia reached for her purse to check the time on her phone.

Holy cow! 2:54 a.m. Yikes.

Then she noticed a text message. It's from Sophia and it was from yesterday. Opening it up, Eugenia read:

> *Aunt Nell and I will be up tomorrow. Catching a plane to Portland then renting a car. Will use the GPS to find your ass. SURPRISE, SURPRISE! Got to meet this man. See you,*
> *Love, Sophia.*

Oh, my God. That means today! I guess I missed that message while at the festival. Okay. It'll be nice to see them and I got plenty of room at the cottage. I really miss them both. It's all good.

Eugenia really had to pee so she went searching for the upstairs bathroom. As she exited the bathroom, she decided to look for Scott. She crept towards his bedroom only to find the door opened. She then glanced in and the light of the street lamp shown across the long arms and legs of Scott. He lay on his back, sprawled across the bed, bare-chested and dressed in only a pair of baggy pajama bottoms, fast asleep. She could faintly see his hairy chest, long arms above his head, and the legs of his 6'3" frame, taking up the entire king size mattress. He slept peacefully.

She watched him for a few minutes feeling like she shouldn't be doing this but stayed nevertheless. *I like this guy, I really do,* she thought. She then made her way downstairs thinking that if she stood there too long, he would awaken. She settled back unto the couch, found a remote control and turned on the television mounted on the back wall, making certain not to have the volume up too loud so as not to wake him. After watching for a while then found herself nodding off, so she turned off the set and resumed her sleep.

The sun rose in Maine this time of the year at around 5 a.m. and the morning light awakened Eugenia out of her slumber. She lay there for a while listening for any sign of Scott moving around upstairs. Nothing. Grabbing the remote control, she turned on the television, flipped through the channels and settled on a show on TV Land.

"Hey, good morning." As she looked up, Eugenia spotted Scott descending the last step, dressed in a burgundy robe that covered up his white pajama bottom. The slight V-neck opening in the robe revealed some dark brown chest hair. She remained covered up in his comforter and greeted him.

"Good morning," she returned the greeting, feeling embarrassed by her falling asleep the night before.

"Scott, I am so sorry that I fell asleep. I feel so...."

"Don't worry about it. I'm glad you're here," he said reassuringly. "How did you sleep?"

"Good. This couch is so comfortable." By this time, he had taken a seat beside her on the couch and sat with his elbows resting on his knees, looking at Eugenia, who was still wrapped up in the comforter, still feeling embarrassed.

"Would you like some breakfast?"

"Oh, no, that's okay. I'd better be going." And at that, she stood up, fished around for her sandals, found them and began to slip them on. Then she looked for her purse.

"Eugenia, please. I'd like to fix you breakfast," Scott pleaded as he watched her gather her things.

Eugenia stood there, purse in hand and shoes on. "I could walk home, it's okay," she said as she started for the front door.

By this time Scott stood up and said sternly. "Eugenia, please, no. I'd like to fix you breakfast, at least coffee and then I will take you home. You're not going out this house without something to eat. Wow, you are stubborn like your father, you know."

Eugenia then looked at him, put her purse down, and kicked her shoes off. She's been told of her stubbornness many times before. She finally conceded. "Well, do you have an extra toothbrush and can I wash up a bit?"

"Yes, I do and, yes, you may. Now that's better. You can take a shower if you want."

"I don't have a change of clothing; I'll wait till I get home."

"Suit yourself."

He told her where the toothbrush was in the upstairs bathroom as well as the linens. He stood and watched her go upstairs. He stood there shaking his head and proceeded into the kitchen to start breakfast.

She came downstairs, found her way into the kitchen and sat at the table for two.

"Is an omelet okay?"

"That's fine."

"Cheese, onions, green peppers and shrimp okay?"

"Wow. That sounds great. I'm glad I stayed." At that, Scott turned around and smiled.

"Blueberry pancakes made with fresh Maine blueberries?"

"Yes, that's great."

Eugenia watched Scott chop, mix, whisk and he looked at home around the kitchen.

"When was dad stubborn?" she asked.

"I'd offer him bowl of chowder every once in a while, a welcome back to Camden when he'd come up. Never took me up on it. Insisted on paying. 'Boy, you can't make money that way giving away food,' he'd say. He was something," Scott said sipping his cup of coffee.

"Yeah, he was stubborn, that's for sure, I know that," as she sipped on the hot, steaming cup of coffee.

"This coffee is great."

"Has a touch of cinnamon."

"It's very good. So, how did you get into the restaurant business?"

"Well, Russ and I, that's one of my partners, we grew up together in D.C. Same neighborhood. He became a lawyer. In fact, he was my divorce lawyer. He told me about the Lobster Fest and Barbara, Chloe and I began coming up here. After the divorce happened, Russ told me about this restaurant right next to the bay that was for sale and he was thinking about buying it. The owners were retiring. I checked it out and it was awesome. So Russ, Cassandra, his wife, and I, decided we'd do this thing. They're both my partners. Cassandra is an attorney, also. And it's worked out pretty good these past three or so years. We're doing something that we clearly enjoy, a nice departure from the rat race that we all experienced in D.C. You'd be surprised at how many people from that area who have settled up here. I've met so many."

Eugenia found herself staring at the coffee cup, her thoughts on relocating here.

"You okay?" Scott turned around after putting some pancakes on the griddle. "You look as though you left me there."

"No, I'm okay."

"Oh, by the way, Cassandra is African American. So they're an interracial couple, like us."

"Oh. Okay. Are we a couple?"

"I sure do hope so." He said jokingly or facetiously. Eugenia didn't know which one.

"I like you, Eugenia." *Actually, I love you.* "We've had some good times." He said as he turned and checked the pancakes.

Eugenia looked up at Scott. "I like you, too," she said.

"Good, despite my corny jokes?"

"In spite of your corny jokes," she said with a half-smile. At that, Scott turned and checked the pancakes. "Good."

Scott put the omelets and pancakes on two plates, put them both on the table, retrieved some butter from the refrigerator, found some syrup in the pantry and poured some orange juice in two glasses. They both dove into their breakfasts.

"Wow, this is really good," Eugenia expressed her approval, tasting both. She then had a gnawing thought that came into her mind that she knew she'd have to reveal to him. She always told any man that she was dating. Eugenia felt that it was time to reveal this fact about her. Here goes.

"Scott, I need to tell you something. It's something that I like to let anyone that I'm dating know early on."

Scott stopped eating and looked at Eugenia with a concerned look on his face. She continued.

"Well," she took a breath, "Here goes — I can't have children. I know we haven't known each other that long, but I feel this is a good time to let you know. I had fibroids, uterine fibroids a few years ago. They got so bad that I had to have a hysterectomy, to have them removed. I just thought I'd let you know, while we're still getting to know one another and this hasn't gotten too serious."

His look of concern disappeared. "I appreciate you telling me. However, I don't want children. Chloe was enough, trust me. I know there are men who have children at my age, but not me. I hate to bring it up again, but that's the problem with dating younger women—they wanted children." Scott continued. "Have you ever wanted children? I mean, I know you don't have any..."

"I guess it wasn't in the cards for me," Eugenia answered bluntly. Scott didn't expect that answer and wanted to press on, but left it at that. It was obvious that she didn't want to talk about it.

They continued their breakfast in silence and then Eugenia broke the stillness. "Oh my goodness, I almost forgot—I got a text from Sophia. She and Aunt Nell are on their way up. I guess she sent it when we were at the festival. They're taking a plane to Portland and then renting a car. Using the GPS, they said they'd find me."

"Really? Wow, that's great! I'd love to meet both of them. Do you have enough room at your cottage?"

"Yeah, one of them could sleep in Daddy's room, another in mine and I could sleep on the pull out bed in the living room."

"Okay. Cause I've got room here, you know. They are more than welcome to stay here."

"Nah. We're good. Thanks."

"I tell you what—I've got to work today, starting at 11. When they arrive, bring them over to Fins, I'll treat them to lunch then for dinner, you guys can come by and I'll throw some steaks on the grill. I'll get wine and we can spend time together and shoot the breeze. How does that sound?"

Eugenia heard the chime from her phone. She went into the living room and retrieved her phone.
We'll be there in a couple of hours. At the airport getting the car. See you, love. It was Sophia.

Eugenia text back, *Do you need directions?* before returning to the kitchen. "They're in Portland getting a car. Oh, Scott that sounds awesome! You don't mind, do you?"

"No, I really want to meet them. Sophia is your friend and Aunt Nell is your relative. Of course, I want to meet them." *They're a part of you, sweetheart.* "I heard a lot from Chuck about his sister. Looking forward to it."

Eugenia glanced again at her phone looking for Sophia's response to her last text message and Scott sat across from her, looking at her. They had finished and Scott then got up to clear the dishes. He then pulled the chair closer to her and sat facing her. Eugenia put her phone on the table. Scott then grabbed her hand, rubbed it and then kissed it.

"I guess you were worried about me wanting to have children."

"Yeah, I was."

"No worries, babe. Has any guy ever left you after you told them and is that why you told me so soon?"

"Yes, that's happened, and yes, that's why I wanted you to know now."

He then put his hand on her cheek. "I can't see why any guy would want to leave you, honest to God. I've enjoyed being with you, I can't even think sometimes." He then gently kissed her on the cheek. "You are such a joy to be around." He then scooted forward in his chair where he had his legs framing hers, moved in closer and placed gentle kisses on her lips. He continued, placing his long arms on her shoulders. She placed her hands under his arms and returned the kisses. After a few minutes, he pulled away and looked into her eyes.

"I really like you, Eugenia. I think of you all the time. I can't wait to see you when we have a date and when you fell asleep on my couch last night, I was so glad that you were here, under my roof, and you'd be staying. I wanted to snuggle up beside you and fall asleep with you."

Wow, thought Eugenia. She liked him, yes, and she thought of him constantly. So she wrapped her arms around his neck and held onto him. Scott then stood up, grabbed Eugenia and held her tightly, rubbing her back. *I want to be here for you, to dry your tears, to laugh with you, to be your friend,* was his thoughts. They then pulled away and Scott kissed her on the forehead.

Scott took Eugenia home, walked her to her door and kissed her in the morning light.

"Let me know, just send me a text when you guys will be coming to Fins, okay?"

"Sure. Thanks so much. They're gonna like that."

"My pleasure." At that, he turned around, got into his SUV and waved goodbye.

Chapter 13

Sophia, Aunt Nell and Maine

Eugenia finally got an answer from her last text to Sophia. *No, we're going to use the GPS. I'll call you if we need directions. Lookin' forward to seeing you and that man!*

Eugenia smiled and texted back, *looking forward to seeing you both.* She took a shower and was about to blow-dry her freshly washed hair when she looked at her roots. *Gotta get a relaxer touch up soon. Don't know where I'm going to get that around here.* She finished her hair, blow drying it, then curling it with the hot curlers.

She got the cottage ready for her arrivals, cleaning up, vacuuming, leaving the paperwork on the coffee table and getting fresh linens for the beds. She had aired out her dad's room where his scent no longer lingered. After making the bed, she sat there for a few minutes thinking about him and reminiscing. *I think he'd be pleased that I am seeing Scott. Wish he was here to see us together.* She then got up, tucked the blankets around the bed and left the room. She no longer cried when thinking about him, only smiled and remembered the lessons he taught her, his smile and the wonderful man that he was.

One could hear the screams and shouts when Sophia and Aunt Nell pulled up to the Sea Street cottage. Eugenia, watching for them, came bursting out the door, running up the sidewalk as Sophia and Aunt Nell got out of the compact rental car.

"Oh, my God, look at you, girl!" screamed Aunt Nell as they hugged. Sophia came from the driver's side and gave Eugenia a hug also.

"You look like a girl in love, look at you," as Sophia pulled away from her and did a once over look.

"Yeah, I guess I kind of look that way," Eugenia said, smiling from ear to ear.

"Yeah, girl, look at you," agreed Aunt Nell.

Miss Martha from next door heard all the commotion and came out onto her porch. Eugenia saw her and introduced the three women to each other. Then she shouted, "We're going over Fins for some lunch later. Would you like to join us?"

"Wow, I haven't been there in a while. Sure, that would be great. Let me know when, okay."

"Okay."

Eugenia then turned to Aunt Nell. "Let me get your bags, come on in." She ushered them into the cottage, asking Aunt Nell how her ankle was holding up. It looked pretty good since she was walking straight again.

Sophia and Aunt Nell settled into their rooms and Eugenia mentioned to them how Scott wanted to treat them all to lunch. They were both looking forward to lunch and meeting Scott as well. They decided to go there around 1 p.m. Eugenia texted Scott and told him what time to expect them there. She asked if it would be okay if Miss Martha joined them. He texted back that it would be great if she joined them. He was looking forward to it and added a smiling emoji to the end of his message.

Aunt Nell and Sophia freshened up and then settled into the living room in front of the coffee table while Eugenia told them about her research and the connection to the little island out in the bay.

"Have you been there yet?" asked Aunt Nell as she sipped on some bottled water.

"No, I haven't. Don't know if they have excursions out there. I'll have to ask Scott, my personal tour guide," she said braggingly.

"What are you going to do with this research?" asked Sophia. "There is an interesting story here."

"Well, I was going to put it together, just for my own personal interest. Scott thought that I need to write it up and make it public."

"Yeah, I agree," said Sophia. "You need to do something more with it. I mean, you can't keep this to yourself. This is a part of local history, African American history."

"Yeah, I know," said Eugenia.

"You know I have had experience in publishing, editing and such. I have contacts back home but can get you in touch with somebody up here in Mayberry, if you want."

Eugenia and Aunt Nell both laughed at the Mayberry reference. "Wow... That sounds great," as the wheels in Eugenia's brain began turning. She told them about the job opportunity at the Rockland Library and how she applied for it.

"So you're planning to stay?" Aunt Nell asked, looking at her seriously, eyebrows raised.

"I think so, Aunt Nell. In this little bit of time, I've grown to like this place."

"It wouldn't have anything to do with a certain man, has it?" asked Aunt Nell.

"Ladies, I am not one of those women who relocates someplace because of a man. But if a job comes along and I can swing it with the income, then I'm going for it."

"I can tell you've given it some thought."

"I have. It's not an easy decision. I would miss you all very much. That's the thing that gets me."

"You have your life to lead, girl. From what I've seen, it's beautiful up here. And we could come visit you, be a great vacation," Aunt Nell justified.

"And you could come back anytime and stay with me," added Sophia. "You'll have to put your condo on the market, unless you're planning on keeping it?"

"No, I would sell it. Don't want the rental thing going on. I could use the proceeds from the sale."
"Yeah, that makes sense. I know some real estate people, as well," added Sophia.

"Who don't you know, Sophia?" and they all laughed. She was one of those people who seemed to know people.

✦ ✦ ✦ ✦ ✦

At a few minutes before one, the four of them, Eugenia, Aunt Nell, Sophia and Miss Martha, piled into Eugenia's SUV and drove down to the restaurant by the bay to enjoy lunch. Megan greeted them and Eugenia and she both hugged each other. Eugenia introduced the ladies to Megan, who seated them and told them she'd be taking care of them this afternoon while giving them all menus. Aunt Nell and Sophia looked around at the quaint restaurant and peered out the windows into Camden Bay at the dozens of boats docked there. Beautiful. A few minutes earlier when they were outside in the restaurant's parking lot, Eugenia pointed out the water falls that was, in her opinion, the most beautiful and unique part of the town. They were in awe of the sight. "You know the movie Peyton Place was filmed here." Both Aunt Nell and Sophia acknowledged that they had seen the movie, filmed back in the 1960s, and vowed to rent it to see it again to check out the scenes.

"I'd like to welcome you to Fins. I am Scott Mackey, part owner of this fine establishment. Please order anything on the menu. It's on me," he said with a wink. "I recommend the chowder, but everything is delicious. You have my word." The four women looked up at the tall, tussled-hair, 45-year-old man with the round glasses and the broad smile. He wore a striped shirt, tucked into a pair of blue jeans. They couldn't help but smile.

Scott bent down, put his arms around Eugenia's shoulders and gave her a quick hug. The other women looked at each other and there were a combination of nods and raised eyebrows. She introduced him to Aunt Nell, who offered her hand but Scott walked around the table and gave her a hug. Eugenia then introduced him to Sophia who, because of her Italian roots, automatically gave him a hug as he walked around the table to greet her. He then hugged Miss Martha, saying that it was good to see her again. "It's been a while," he stated.

"Yes, it has. It looks as though you've been doing well for yourself," Miss Martha replied.

"Yes, ma'am, I have," he answered with a quick wink. He excused himself saying something about getting back into the kitchen. As soon as he turned to leave and had gotten a few feet from the table, he heard screams coming from the ladies' table. The screams, led by Sophia, were screams that the women approved of Scott. He walked into the kitchen, smiling to himself, shaking his head.

Megan took their drink orders and they all ordered chowder while looking at the choice of entrees. Megan returned with their drinks and a person from the kitchen brought over a tray of chowders. They all chatted about various things. Eugenia looked around at the now-crowded restaurant and figured she would not see much of Scott who was probably attending to the many customers who now packed the place. They all stopped talking as they heard the sound of the keys on the piano.

"This one's for you, Eugenia…," was the voice of Scott on the microphone, breaking through the noise of the voices of the restaurant patrons. He then played "Wonderful Tonight" by Eric Clapton, the same song that he played the first night she was at Fins. However, this time he sang the words. They all listened in silence, staring at Eugenia, who looked over towards the piano mesmerized.

After he finished, the applause rang out, everyone cheering. Scott then played an instrumental version of "All I Ask of You" from the Phantom of the Opera, and the audience loved it. Scott came back on the microphone and announced the next song.

"This is 'Stairway to the Stars' and this is for you Chuck." He played the song that Eugenia knew was one of her dad's favorites. Looking over at Aunt Nell, Eugenia saw her dabbing tears from her eyes. Aunt Nell ended up smiling, thinking about how happy Eugenia looked and remembering her younger brother. Again, applause. Scott stopped playing and the women either laughed or teased Eugenia.

"How romantic is that to be sung to?" chimed in Miss Martha, "And I like it when he dedicated that song to Chuck. That was really special." They continued to talk, eat and drink. Then Eugenia felt a pair of hands on her shoulders.

"Did you enjoy that?" he asked.

"Very nice," said Sophia, dragging nice out.

"That was very nice, young man," said Aunt Nell, still dabbing her eyes still. "That was one of Charles' favorites and I appreciate you playing it."

"It was my pleasure, Aunt Nell."

Eugenia then looked up at Scott, "Thank you so much."

He bent down and whispered, "The pleasure was all mine, babe," and kissed her on the cheek.

"Well, look, I've got to go. We're getting swamped." He then bent down slightly and addressed Eugenia. "Are we still on for tonight?"

He then addressed the group of women. "I wanted you ladies to come over to my place. I'm going to throw some steaks on the grill, have some drinks and then we can play Twister." Aunt Nell suddenly looked up with a shocked look.

"He's kidding, Aunt Nell. Just for steaks and drinks, that's all," clarified Eugenia. They all burst out laughing.

"I was going to say, not with my bursitis," chuckled Aunt Nell.

"Do you ladies like any particular liquor, wine?" Scott asked.

"Moscato," said Eugenia. The others agreed that was fine.

"Cristal, Remy Martin Louis the 13th. Can you manage that?" piped in Aunt Nell, not cracking a smile.

"You have expensive taste, Aunt Nell."

"Payback for scaring me with that Twister stuff!" said Aunt Nell with a straight face. Then she burst out laughing and everyone else joined in.

"Well, okay, you got me. No more Twister jokes. See you ladies, say seven? And you're coming also, Miss Martha?"

"Sure, why not."

"Then it's settled, seven at my place." Scott bent down and kissed Eugenia on the cheek. "See you later, babe," he whispered.

"I'll see you," answered Eugenia. She then watched him as he walked towards the kitchen. When she turned her attention back to the ladies at the table, she exclaimed, "What?"

"He's cuuuuuuuuuute," piped in Sophia. "Somebody has goo-goo eyes for him. I told Eugenia that she needed to come up here and jump in the sack with that sexy man. But I guess she didn't take my advice?"

Eugenia turned to Miss Martha, not knowing if Sophia's comments offended her or not.

"Miss Martha, excuse my friend over here. We have some colorful conversations at times…"

"Eugenia, I'm a big girl. At my age, I've heard it all, and maybe even done it all." They all looked at one another with a look of approval. "Now, Sophia, what were you saying about jumping in the sack? I want details." The other ladies turned and looked at each other, shrugged and laughed.
Aunt Nell piped in, "Now that's what I'm talking about. Let's drink up and talk some more trash." Clinking their glasses together, they all laughed and realized that they were on the same page as far as the way the conversation was going.

During the toast, Eugenia was suddenly aware of what she had—three women of various ages and backgrounds, coming together in this beautiful town, celebrating being women, talking trash and having fun. Just a few weeks ago, she was feeling alone, scared and uncertain about her future. Sophia was right—you never know what's around the corner, and it's up to you as to what you're going to do with it.

Since the layoff, Eugenia discovered her family, tapped into history, rediscovered a beautiful town, gotten to know her father more, and met an apparently fantastic man who sings to her! Who would have thought! The women toasted to new beginnings, discovery and exploring what's to come. They toasted themselves.

The four women arrived to the aroma of wood burning and steaks on the grill. Eugenia led them past the motorcycle to the backyard passing the side of the house. In the center of the concrete patio sat a beige colored rectangular wooden table surrounded by six matching chairs. An eggshell colored umbrella was anchored in the center of the table and was open providing shade from the evening sun that was beginning its slow descent in the western sky. The sturdy chairs each had a seat cushion. There were flowers blooming in large clay pots making up the perimeter of the patio. The pots contained impatiens of several colors including white and various shades of pink. There were several chaise lounge chairs on the patio that matched the table and chair set and each had a seat cushion. The backyard had a few pine trees that made up the border of the property backing up to neighboring yards. Scott, donning a chef's apron with the Fins logo on the front, a spatula in hand, was standing by the grill. All of the women wanted a tour of the house and he let Eugenia know to take the ladies in.

"Be my guest."

Entering through the back door, Eugenia showed the ladies the kitchen, plush living room, and dining area before taking them upstairs to show them the rest of the house.

"And here's the den of iniquity," touted Sophia, referring to the bedroom. "This is nice. I like the king size bed. You know, Eugenia, I could suggest ten things you could do in that bed with Scott and all of them would be illegal in both Maryland and Maine," as she practically pushed Eugenia into his room. They all looked at Sophia and burst out laughing.

"I know, Sophia, I know that you could and would," she assured Sophia. They all laughed.

"Shit, I would've had that hunk..."

"Sophia! He might be downstairs, hearing all this…Shhhh."

"I don't care. You know I don't. And the man sings to you? Shit." They all continued to laugh and glanced into the bedroom, nodding their heads in approval.

After the tour, they settled outside in the backyard occupying the chairs set up around a table. Eugenia grabbed a bottle of wine out of the refrigerator and Scott gave them all glasses, opened the bottle and poured the wine. They all raised their glasses and Scott proposed a toast, standing by Eugenia who was seated.

"To Eugenia." As he looked down at her, all of the others' eyes were on both of them. "I'm just going to say it. I know you've been back and forth, grabbling with the thought, but…," he then paused and swallowed, "I hope you can stay." And with that, they all clinked the glasses together and took a sip. Eugenia and Scott's eyes locked on one another. Eugenia said nothing as Scott bent down, kissed her on the cheek, put his glass down and went over to resume his grilling.

Eugenia got up, excused herself and went into the house to go to the downstairs bathroom. She shut the door and then looked at herself in the mirror. *Why does he keep reminding me? I want to stay but I don't have a job,* she thought. *Can't he get that into his head?* The tears welled up in her eyes. She was scared, just plain scared. The thought of staying here, not employed, not earning a living, the money running out, and the uncertainty flooded her mind and she began to cry. The fear gripped her and came to a head.

After a few minutes, Eugenia gathered herself together. She dried her tears, blew her nose and looked in the mirror once again. Her eyes were red and she then dabbed them with some cold water, hoping to get rid of the evidence that she had cried. No luck. She did the best she could. *Hopefully nobody will notice.* And with that, went out to face her friends.

As she walked through the kitchen, Scott was in the refrigerator taking a couple of dishes of salad out to take them out to his guests. Eugenia tried to get pass him without making any eye contact. No luck.

"You all right, babe?"

"Yeah, fine," still avoiding his eyes and trying to get outside. "Did you need some help? Let me grab one of these bowls." She then pried one out of Scott's hands and continued onto the patio. She put the bowl onto the table and everyone stopped talking. Scott was right behind her and decided to leave her alone. He would ask later.

One by one, the guests grabbed a plate, got a steak from the grill, and feasted on homemade rolls, pasta and green salads. Scott joined the ladies

at the table and everyone complimented the chef on the food.
"I had one of my chefs throw together the salads. Pretty good, huh?"

The lively talk continued into the evening. They stayed out after the sun had set since Scott had plenty of lighting on the patio. While enjoying the warm Maine summer evening, their conversation ran the gamut—from talking about Chuck to the goings on back in D.C. Miss Martha made a comment that she hadn't had this much fun since the 1960s. She had been to the Woodstock Music Festival and everyone leaned forward to hear about her experience during that event. Aunt Nell spoke of raising Eugenia and how she helped her brother with everything needed to bring up a female child. Scott listened intently; he wanted to know everything he could about Eugenia.

Eugenia continued to be silent and occasionally laughed, but not like everyone else. She had had quite a bit to drink and instead of making her feel lighthearted, she stayed silent. She was scared. She was so scared of her uncertain future. No one could get her out of that mood, no joke seemed to work, no amount of laughter could shake it.

Since Eugenia was in no condition to drive, even for that short distance, Scott insisted on driving the ladies back to the cottage. They all piled into Scott's SUV and headed to Sea Street. When they pulled up to the cottage, Sophia got Eugenia's keys and they all left Eugenia and Scott in the SUV, Eugenia saying goodbye to Miss Martha. Eugenia was looking straight ahead, not looking at Scott after everyone had exited the vehicle. Scott looked over at her but she didn't look at him.

"Eugenia, look at me," he said sternly. She finally turned to face him, noticing his round glasses in the darkness with only the light of the streetlamp to illuminate his face. She also saw the puzzled expression on his face and the look of worry.

"What is wrong? Did I say anything?"

She then started to turn to exit the car. Scott reached out to grab her arm. "Babe, please…," he pleaded. Eugenia stopped and closed the half-opened door, settling back into the car seat.

"I've told you I don't know if I can stay. You keep reminding me of that. I just don't know…," and with that Eugenia began to sob. Scott then reached over, put his arms around her, pulled her tightly toward him and held her in his arms. She continued to softly cry on his shoulders. After a few minutes, she stopped and pulled away. Scott reached over across her lap and retrieved some tissues from the glove compartment. He gave them to Eugenia and she dried her eyes and blew her nose. Using more tissues, Scott dabbed her eyes and wiped her face. He knew how much he wanted her to stay and wanted to tell her that. But instead, he left it alone. He didn't say anything realizing that it may make things worse. They both sat there in silence, Scott occasionally kissing her on the forehead or giving her a hug. He grabbed her hand and kissed it, not knowing what to say or do to ease her mind or reassure her. He, too, knew of her uncertainty. How can she stay here? He wanted to take care of her, to protect her. His feelings for her were of love and of caring. He knew he loved this woman and felt helpless as to an answer to her dilemma. She'd have to figure this one out and he would help in any way that he could.

He then began, recalling a previous conversation, "Eugenia, you'd mentioned that you wanted to go to Mass on Sunday. Did you still want to go tomorrow? There's a 10 o'clock Mass. I'd like to take you." She looked over at Scott and nodded. "Then I'll pick you up at around 9:30?"

"Yes, that would be fine." And at that, Eugenia leaned over and kissed Scott on the lips. Scott placed his hand on her cheek, kissed her once again before Eugenia turned to open the door and exit the car.

"Wait," said Scott, as he got out of the car, rushed around to the passenger side and opened her door. They said their goodnights and Eugenia walked on down the path to the cottage and Scott watched her walk inside the unlocked door. Scott got into his car and left.

Once inside, Eugenia told Aunt Nell and Sophia what was going on. They knew that she was scared and they offered their opinions. They were all pretty tired and decided to turn in for the night. Eugenia mentioned that she'd be going to Mass in the morning.

Chapter 14

Camden Bay and Negro Island Lighthouse

S unday mornings were always special to Eugenia because it marked the beginning of a new week and this week was quite different. It could be the start of a new beginning or it could be a week where she prepared to return to Maryland. After all, this was supposed to be her last week in Maine, at least until she decided at some point in the future to return to the cottage on vacation. She was hoping that she would hear from the library about an interview. She planned to do more research to find out more about her ancestors. And what about Scott?

Eugenia jumped into the shower after sleeping a little longer than she had intended and was running late. The other two ladies were still asleep. She brushed her hair and put it in a bun. She then slipped on a sleeveless, white dress that gathered at the waist and flowed out from the waist to about mid-calf. She wrapped a wide black belt around her waist and the dress took shape. She slid into a pair of white wedged, open-toe shoes. Her earrings were gold hoops and she wore some mascara and a dark hue of red lipstick. After taking a look in the mirror, Eugenia went into the living room to wait for Scott. At around 9:30, she heard that all-too-familiar knock on the door. She opened the door to an even more handsome Scott than she had seen before. *I guess it's the suit.* He wore a beautiful navy blue fitted single-breasted suit with a striped tie and white shirt. He stood there with his hands in his pocket, hair a bit tussled, neatly trimmed beard and glasses with a look on his face that said, hopefully she's okay today. For the first few seconds, Eugenia took all of this in and could say nothing, and taking a breath, she breathed in that now-familiar soapy scent that was all

Scott. *Wow!*

"Good morning," said Scott. "Wow. You look beautiful," almost in a whisper. He was so unsure. *Should I kiss her? I don't know what to do*, he thought, trying to discern her mood.

"Good morning. You look really good, too." She grabbed her purse on the table by the door and grabbed the key to lock up. She had left the spare key so that if Sophia and Aunt Nell wanted to venture out, they could. Scott opened the door to the SUV and Eugenia got in. The conversation was more small talk—how was your evening, how did you sleep. There was a lot of silence with Eugenia occasionally looking over at Scott, marveling at the suit and the entire package. Wow!

Our Lady of Good Hope Catholic Church was a beautiful white church with a steeple. They entered, made the sign of the cross using the traditional dish of holy water by the door, genuflected and took a seat in a pew near the front of the church. After saying prayers using the kneeler, they sat down and waited for the Mass to begin. Scott took Eugenia's hand and held it. *Well, she's not pulling away. That's good.* Scott was still trying to gauge her mood. *So far, so good.* He continued to hold it, occasionally squeezing it.

The priest's homily was about faith. He tied it into the preceding Bible readings. Eugenia tried to take in everything he was saying and how faith was the belief in something not based on truth, based on something intangible, something that you couldn't reach out and touch—but was still there. She began thinking of her situation. Should she stay here and make a go of it, facing the unknown, the uncertainty, but a potential of a different life? Or should she leave and return to the familiarity and comfort of her former life in Maryland, which would still have a degree of uncertainty? She began to think of the possibility of staying in Maine and equated it to a leap of faith. However, sometimes faith was hard to fathom. After being laid off, having had faith in a company that ended up not valuing what she had—it was hard to grasp such a concept. She continued to listen, continued to think, continued to believe.

Eugenia focused on what she had. She was the product of a group of beautiful, proud black women whose story should be told. She remembered the picture of the five generations of women, her ancestors, from whom she descended. She was raised by a good man who always told her to hold her head up, instilling in her pride, honor, and the belief she could be anything she wanted to be. She just had to "put her mind to it" as her dad would say. She had Aunt Nell who taught her how to be a lady and a woman. She had a talent—she could put her ideas down on paper with little effort and tell a story. She had a gift and she now realized that fact, even though it's always been there.

As they left the church, Scott never let go of her hand. He asked her if she was hungry, if she'd eaten breakfast. She shook her head and Scott offered to cook her breakfast.

"Does it include blueberry pancakes?" she asked as they drove through town.

"Yes, I can whip some up."

"Okay, you got a deal." Eugenia made a call to Sophia to let her know that she was going to Scott's for breakfast. Scott then chimed in, "And they are more than welcome to join us."

Sophia and Aunt Nell got into the rental car and found their way over to his house. They sat down to pancakes, omelets and fruit while enjoying the lively conversation. Eugenia seemed happier and more content and Scott took notice. He couldn't help but stare at this beautiful woman sitting at his dining room table, laughing at some of Sophia's stories. Perhaps it was the homily at church, maybe the night's sleep. But she seemed more like herself this Sunday morning.

Scott mentioned that he was working some of the day but offered to take the ladies on a boat tour of the harbor. He turned to Eugenia sitting to his left at the dining room table and said, "My buddy has one of the boats right there by the restaurant. He takes tourists out every day. You'll be able to see Curtis Island Lighthouse. I'd like to show you that." He then took her hand as Aunt Nell and Sophia stopped talking and looked on.

"I'd like to see that," she added. Eugenia was finally going to see the island that she'd been researching and the subject of the several paintings and photos that donned the walls of the cottage. *I'm actually going to see it,* was her thoughts. *And this man is going to take me there. What a sweetheart!*

Later that afternoon, after Scott got off from work, he met the ladies at the pier and they climbed onto the boat that had the capacity to seat about 20 people. It was a small tourist boat complete with seats that faced forward like a classroom. The front several rows of seats were under an overhang and the back seats had no shade and exposed to the sun. Eugenia, Aunt Nell, Sophia, and Scott got seats up front and Scott introduced them to the Captain, a weathered, middle-aged man wearing a captain's hat, and his first mate, a young woman in her 20s. Both sported skin tones indicating that they had spent long hours in the sun and their complexions were slightly darker than Eugenia's. As the first mate unhooked the necessary ropes that attached the boat to the pier, they set sail on the boat, accompanied by a total of 15 or so passengers. Scott and Eugenia sat in the front two seats on the starboard side and Sophia and Aunt Nell sat in seats on the opposite side of the aisle, on the port side. The afternoon sun shone brightly and the four of them sported sunglasses.

The Captain, who was also the tour guide, spoke with a typical Maine accent, not seeming to know about the letter "r" in some words. Using his microphone, he informed his audience of the many beautiful attractions that Camden Bay offered. He talked about the celebrities who once had summer homes in Camden, pointing to some of the homes situated off in the distance on shore. He showed everyone the many lobster traps that dotted the waters. As they pulled away from the shore, Mount Battie stood behind them off in the distance behind Camden proper. What a beautiful sight—Camden, Maine, was truly a town where the mountains meet the sea. The Captain's description was all well and good; however, Eugenia, who tried to listen, found her eyes glued in the direction of the Curtis Island Lighthouse that had yet to come into view. Scott pointed in the direction and promised it was coming. Although Eugenia was enjoying the beauty of Camden and its uniqueness, she anxiously awaited her first glimpse of the lighthouse.

The Captain finally steered the boat to the right and after making a second turn, the island, with its rocky shoreline, appeared off to the right. Eugenia's eyes lit up as she stared in that direction. First, the lighthouse came into view. There it stood, the top portion of the lighthouse was black and it looked as though there was some sort of walkway that encircled the top part of the white building. Their boat circled and Eugenia saw the keeper's house, a white one-story structure sporting a red, gabled roof. The house sat next to the lighthouse. Once they got closer, the Captain stopped the boat and turned off the engine, so that everyone could take pictures and get a better view. Eugenia and Scott posed for pictures as Sophia snapped a photo of both of them with the island and the lighthouse in the background. Then Scott shot pictures of Eugenia alone, with the structure in the background.

Eugenia then ceased the picture taking and just stared at the island. She found herself leaning against the inside of the boat, as if wanting to jump into the water and swim to get closer to the island. She experienced the same feeling that she got when she found out the identities of the women on the hand-written list in the scrapbook. There was a sense of familiarity even though she had never met those women. She knew she had a connection. She knew that this was a part of her—a part that she had discovered and unknown up until recently. This overwhelming feeling was so new to her and caught her by surprise. Eugenia could feel tears welling up in her eyes and she removed her sunglasses and began wiping her tears.

Scott looked at her as she wiped her eyes and whispered, "I wondered how you would react. I know, it has to be emotional. You have ties here. That was his island." Eugenia had her back to him, still looking at the island. Scott sat behind her, wrapped his arms around her shoulders, bringing her close to him and holding her tightly. No one else seemed to notice, all too preoccupied with taking pictures and talking about the island, except for Sophia and Aunt Nell, who watched them both. As the Captain talked about the island, there was no mention of its former name, Negro Island. There was no mention of her ancestor or his story. Nothing.

The Captain started up the boat and began the trek back to the shore. Eugenia continued to stare at the island until it was out of sight. The Captain resumed his explanation of the sights on the bay. After Eugenia had finished wiping her eyes, she then turned to Scott and looked at him. She then spilled out her thoughts and she seemed to talk at a hundred miles an hour. With fierce determination in her voice, she said,

"Scott, I'm going to write Ezekiel Freeman's story. I'm going to find out about all those women listed in that scrapbook. I'm going to do that. Scott, I hope I can get that job at the library. But if I don't, I'm going to keep looking and, in the meantime, I'm going to write down, document and tell the story of my ancestors. It needs to be told. You're right—there isn't a lot of African American history here and I intend to change that."

Scott listened intently stuck on every word and in awe of her determination. He saw in her a strength of mind and purpose that he had not witnessed in her before. He loved her even more now than ever. He then took her into his arms and hugged her. He then pulled away and looked at her.

"I know you can do this. You have it in you…." Then he stopped, digesting what she had just said and continued, "Whoa, wait a minute—are you saying what I think you're saying? Are you going to stay here, in Maine, in Camden?"

"Yes. Yes, I am," she said, smiling.

"Okay, Eugenia, don't joke about this, please."

She looked at him squarely in the eye and repeated it. "I'm staying here. Yes, you heard right."

Still skeptical, Scott continued. "You're not pulling my leg, are you? You're really serious, right?"

"Yes, Scott, I'm dead serious."

"Okay, dead serious is good. Oh, my God, Eugenia, you have made me the happiest man. Oh, my God." And in front of everyone on the boat, he wrapped his arms around her and gently kissed her on her lips. He then pulled away and looked at her. "Thank you," he said.

"For what?" asked Eugenia.

"For making me so happy." He then put his long arm around her shoulders and held her there until they reached the shore.

By now Sophia and Aunt Nell had moved behind them and Eugenia turned to tell them the news. As the waves splashed up on the moving boat, both women screamed out shouts of joy. Sophia reiterated what she had told Eugenia about her contacts in publishing and in real estate; Aunt Nell hugged her, telling her how much she was going to miss her.

The celebration continued at the cottage where Eugenia decided to treat the group to her stir-fry recipe for dinner. Scott went home to change into a pair of blue jeans, a white Fins tee shirt and sandals, and he brought some wine, homemade bread from the restaurant, and the biggest smile, over to the cottage. Eugenia, now in a pair of shorts, tank top, with her hair down and barefoot, stood in the kitchen slicing the vegetables and cooking the chicken. Scott helped while Sophia and Aunt Nell were packing for their return to Maryland, each in their respective bedrooms. Their trip back included an early morning drive back to Portland. From there they would board a plane bound for BWI, ending their glorious time in Camden, Maine.

Pandora radio played in the background in Eugenia's kitchen and she found herself singing to some of the songs on the radio.

"You know, you have a nice voice," said Scott, as he took a break from the chopping and sat at the kitchen table, sitting with his ankle of one of his long legs resting on the opposite knee. He sat comfortably, looking at Eugenia, a glass of wine sitting on the table.

"Thank you. But it's more suitable for the shower."

"I could see you belting out an Ella Fitzgerald song, maybe even an Etta James tune. You have that range, you know."

"Okay, you're not going to suggest what I think you're going to suggest, are you?"

"And what would that be, pray tell?" Scott said teasingly.

She stopped chopping some mushrooms, turned to Scott and said, "That I sing at Fins? That I accompany you at the piano? That I slip on a tight fitting, black dress, or red, and stand beside the piano while you play 'Someone to Watch Over Me', or some other Ella Fitzgerald tune? And the audience would applaud wildly. And we'd attract an audience every night. And our popularity would soar. Is that what you were thinking?"

Scott went silent before looking at Eugenia with a serious look.

"Exactly."

Eugenia, with the one hand that didn't contain the knife on her hip, stared at Scott in disbelief, scowling with her eyes.

"You're shittin', right?"

"Eugenia, it's Sunday and we just went to Mass this morning. Please," he said half smiling. She continued to stare, hand on hip.

"You're dead serious, aren't you?"

"Yes, I am. I could pay you. That part of our relationship could be the business part. You'd probably get tips galore. Think about it…please?"

Still staring at him, she added, "Wow. Okay, I'll think about it." *Geez, me a lounge singer? Is he kidding?*

"That's all I ask. You know you have the fiercest stare I have ever seen. It really reminds me of Chuck. It really sends chills through me. Just wanted you to know that."

"Yeah. How about that? I remember it, too. It was usually followed by 'Eugenia Ann, I'm really disappointed in you.' Yeah that was Dad." A smile came to Eugenia's face as she turned to continue chopping and thoughts about her dad going through her head. Good thoughts. Fond memories.

"Oh, that's your middle name? Nice. Well, I think a tight, red dress would be good. Kind of short, but not too short," moving his hands to indicate the length. "I'd like to see those legs," Scott said with a slight smirk on his face. Eugenia turned to him again, rolled her eyes and laughed.

She added, "Yes, we were just in Mass this morning, smarty," and they both laughed. Scott, still trying to picture Eugenia in such a dress, kept the rest of his thoughts to himself. *She is sexy; she is beautiful.*

"What's your middle name, smart ass?" she asked.

"James."

"Okay, Jimmy, I think everything's almost ready. Can you set the table?"

"Yes, ma'am."

✦ ✦ ✦ ✦ ✦

Enjoying their last meal in Camden, Aunt Nell and Sophia joined Scott and Eugenia at the kitchen table in Eugenia's kitchen. *Wow, this is really nice,* Eugenia thought. *I love these people.* She realized that she loved all of them, even Scott. She took a swig of her wine and watched Scott as he explained life at Fins to Aunt Nell and Sophia. He was so handsome, using animated gestures with his hands to get his point across, smiling with that bright smile and that easy laugh and intermittently adjusting his eyeglasses on his nose. Occasionally he'd look over at Eugenia with a wink and a grin. And as they sat at the kitchen table sipping the wine and finishing up Eugenia's delicious stir-fry over rice, she reflected upon the people sitting in her kitchen.

The thought of staying here still scared Eugenia but she was determined to give it a shot and take a leap of faith. She knew she had a great support system. She had looked at her finances and gotten everything lined up and in order. The thought of researching and writing her family history and the African American history of this area excited her to no end. Eugenia even had a good feeling about the library job and she should hear about that this week. She felt that she was on better footing. Thanks to her support system, to that man that everyone called Chuck, who instilled in her pride and confidence in herself, she knew she had a foothold onto her future.

And Scott? Somehow he fitted nicely into this equation. *I never would have thought that not even a week ago, when he came over to my table and introduced himself, that it would be like this. I could listen to him for hours, could look at him even longer because he is so cute! And the piano playing? That's just the epitome of romance. Geez.*

Somehow the fact that he was white didn't matter, although she was acutely aware that there were stares, gawking, and ogling; she noticed this especially when they first started going out. She noticed the looks, the looks of judgment in peoples' faces. But her awareness of these narrow-minded people had subsided. It really didn't matter. And it appeared that Scott never ever noticed.

The evening wore on and Aunt Nell offered to wash the dishes but Eugenia wasn't having it. As she stayed behind to clean up the kitchen, the two ladies wanted to turn in early because they had to wake at the ungodly hour of 3 a.m. Eugenia continued to wash the dishes and clean while the others went into the living room. She could hear their conversations since both Aunt Nell and Sophia seemed to talk a few decibels above anyone else that Eugenia ever knew. Eugenia smiled at this fact as she dried the dishes. "Yeah, I've got to get back to work on Tuesday," Aunt Nell added. "I think I've pushed this ankle thing long enough, milked it for all it's worth. The doctor said to use my own judgment as to when I thought I should go back to work. So, that's what I did." They all laughed.

"Yeah, I've got to get back to retirement," injected Sophia. The conversation continued but Eugenia noticed that things got quiet. She didn't think much of it as she dried off the kitchen counter and put the dishes away, although it was unusual for both of the ladies. She went about her tasks, making sure the kitchen was clean. When she finally finished, she came through the kitchen door and heard,

"Oh, I intend to...," Scott said as Eugenia came out of the kitchen with a dish rag still over her shoulder, obviously walking in on a conversation.

"Intend to do what?" she asked.

"I asked Scott to take care of my baby girl," said Aunt Nell with a most serious look on her face, wiping her eyes a bit, as if fighting back tears.

"Oh?" said Eugenia, still observing the looks on each of their faces. No one was giving up an explanation. No one said anything.

Hmmm, thought Eugenia.

As Aunt Nell and Sophia said their goodbyes to Scott, they both hugged him. Afterwards, they retreated to their rooms. The couple then settled down on Eugenia's couch. She became aware of just how it wasn't as comfortable as Scott's L-shape sectional and vowed to buy some new furniture as soon as it was possible. The uncomfortable couch briefly distracted Eugenia. She wanted to ask Scott about the looks on her loved ones faces when she first walked into the living room. She decided to leave it alone. *Perhaps Aunt Nell was wiping her eyes because she was going to miss me. I'm sure going to miss her.*

"How's it going, babe?"

Eugenia remembered Scott's comments to Aunt Nell and asked defiantly, "Are you going to take care of me? Because you know how I'm an independent woman, I've always been on my own, I..."

"Whoa. Hold up...Eugenia, I want to be someone that you can depend on, someone that will be beside you, to support you. I want to be your friend, which I thought I already was. I want to be your man."
Eugenia looked at him and answered, "I know. It's been a long time since I met someone as sincere as you. Sometimes you seem too good to be true, starting with your piano playing. Sometimes you don't seem real. It's been a long time, so excuse me while I adjust to this...everything."

Scott looked at her squarely in the eyes. "Babe, this is real. I'm the real thing. I've told you I'm tired of the games and the lies. You've been honest with me and I know you're tired of the games as well. I'm sincere. I'm the real deal. Eugenia, I love you. I was attracted to you when I saw you that first time, sitting at that table back in the corner. And I am so glad I was able to take you out and show you Maine. That night we met, I was so frightened that I wouldn't see you again and that you would not come back to the restaurant. And when you came that next night, I was just so elated, I could barely think straight. I love you and I'm so glad you're staying."

He grabbed her and hugged her more tightly than he had ever before. Eugenia held onto to him as well. As they pulled away, Scott kissed her on her lips even more passionately than ever. Eugenia returned the kisses and they continued for a few more minutes.

Scott sat on the driver's side of his SUV with the door open, hanging out the car, coaxing Eugenia to come closer as he sat legs spread where she could fit in between them. As she stood between his long legs, he used them to grip her hips and held her in place. Scott held onto her tightly and Eugenia wrapped her arms around his waist. Her head lay on his chest and Scott rubbed her back and caressed her as the warm Maine breeze occasionally kicked up, finding its way through the darkness of the night.

"Can we stay like this forever?" begged Scott as he held onto her tightly.

Gosh, this feels so good, thought Eugenia. Scott then pulled away from her.

"What are your plans for tomorrow, babe?"

"Probably get back online and look again for jobs in this area."

"I like the way that sounds, in the area."

"Hopefully I'll hear from the Rockland library. I've got to see about selling my condo and begin wrapping up things back home. Wow, that sounds weird, back home."

"Yeah, I know, babe," he said as he tucked Eugenia's hair behind one ear.

"Well, we're closed tomorrow."

"Oh, I thought you opened seven days a week. You've been opened since I've been here."

"No, that's only during Lobster Fest. We close Mondays and Tuesdays during the rest of the year. I've got so much to do around the house, so I'll be home all day. Got gutters to be cleaned, look at some plumbing stuff, the usual house stuff."

"Yeah, I'm going to see Aunt Nell and Sophia off in the morning and probably will try to go back to sleep. Then I'll do my usual walk in the morning."

"Maybe I'll run into you during my run."

"Oh, you run?"

"Yeah, haven't done too much lately with the restaurant. But, yeah, I run."

Once again, he pulled her close. He whispered, "I'd like for you to come over tonight, but I know you have to see your folks off tomorrow." He looked at her, pushing her hair behind her ear. "I just loved it when you were there the other night. Even though you were downstairs, the fact that you were there when I woke up, that was great. I find myself missing you when you're away from me. Does that sound strange?"

"I think of you a lot, too. I really do." *Gosh, you are too sexy,* thought Eugenia.

They finally tore away from each other and Eugenia waited by the door of the cottage, waving goodbye, standing there until he got out of sight before going inside. She prepared the sofa bed for her uncomfortable night's sleep and went to the bathroom to get ready for bed. As she lay in the darkened room, illuminated only by the streetlamp shining through the window, she nestled under the covers in her night shirt and thought of how it would be to lie in his bed, beside him and wrapped up in his arms. She imagined how it would be to make love to him. She knew she wanted him and he wanted her. *Why can't I tell him that I love him? Does it scare me that much? Have I been hurt so much that I can't feel that way? Did Jamal hurt me that much?*

It took her what seemed like forever to get over Jamal and it had been over a year since they broke up. *He was so fine and he knew it. He had to have another woman. Why didn't I get out? Why did I hang around—to try to win him back? What a fool I was! But he never said that he loved me, he never made me feel like Scott does. Lord, knows, I loved him, that's for sure. I must have told him a million times and it didn't matter. I couldn't make him love me and that was my mistake.*
But this is definitely different with Scott. Should I take a leap of faith with Scott?

She lay there until finally falling asleep with thoughts of Scott filling her dreams.

Chapter 15

Faith

Eugenia woke to Sophia and Aunt Nell trying to leave quietly as not to wake up their niece and friend. But it didn't work. Eugenia got up, saw them off, curled back onto the sofa bed, fell asleep and continued the Scott-dream marathon. In one dream, they were getting married in St. Mary's Church in Rockville, Md. She and her dad had visited that church many times and she remembered its unique round shape. *How did I get back there?* she thought as she awakened from that dream.

She decided not to walk that morning but instead got online and continued her job search—now concentrating on the Rockland-Camden-Portland areas. It's scary but at the same time exciting. Just then she heard a chime from her phone indicating a text message. It was Scott.

Good morning. I hope you slept well. Hopefully I'll see you later today? Like to take you to lunch, dinner, both? Please let me know. Miss and love you, babe. Scott.

How sweet. Instead of texting him back, she called him.

"I thought I'd do something old fashioned and speak to you over the phone. How are you?" asked Eugenia.

"I couldn't be better. How are you?"

"Well, I slept on that pull out couch and it was pretty uncomfortable. Other than that, I'm okay."

"I can imagine it's pretty uncomfortable. Can I treat you to lunch today?"

"I thought you were working on your house today?" Then Eugenia noticed a call coming in and she then said, "Wait, Scott, I got another call. Hold on." She then clicked in on the call.

"Hello?" not recognizing the phone number on the display.

"Yes, good morning. Is this Eugenia Watts?" the stranger's voice said.

"Yes, it is."

"This is Pat Gaines from the Rockland Library. How are you? We met a few days ago."

"Oh, yes. I'm good. How are you?"

"Good. Did you have a good weekend?" she asked.

"Yes, saw a little more of the area. Very nice."

"Good. Well, the reason I'm calling is I'd like to bring you in for an interview for the library historian position. Sorry for the short notice, but can you come in this afternoon, say 3 o'clock?"

Eugenia stood in the middle of her living room and couldn't move, couldn't speak, was completely caught off guard.

"Ms. Watts, are you still there?"

"Oh, yes. I'm still here. I'm sorry. Um, yes, I can." And for a split second, all the things she needed to do quickly sped through her mind. "Um, yes. At the Rockland Library?"

"Yes, when you come into the library, just ask the person at the desk to call me and I'll come to meet you, okay?"

"Yes, I'll see you there. Thank you so much."

"You're quite welcome. See you then."

She then hung up the phone briefly and forgot that Scott was on the other line. She then clicked in, "Scott!" she said shouting.

"What...," Scott responded, both puzzled and concerned at Eugenia's sudden exuberance.

"I have an interview at 3 o'clock today at the Rockland Library. Didn't think I'd hear from them this quickly."

"Oh, my God, that's great!" he exclaimed.

"I have so much to do, iron my suit, comb my hair, make-up...Oh, my God!"

"Eugenia calm down, babe. Now take a breath. I can tell you're pacing back and forth. Please stop."

How did he know that?

She stood there in the middle of her living room and stopped pacing. She stood still and breathed as instructed. "Okay, I'm good."

"Okay. You good?"

"Yes."

"I got a proposal—why don't I bring you some lunch and we can rehearse the interview. I interview people at the restaurant, and I could give you pointers. How's that?"

"Oh sure. I could use your help."

"Now that's what I'm talking about. You see, I'm a useful guy."

Eugenia smiled. "Okay, look, give me an hour or so. I haven't even taken a shower and I gotta iron some clothes. Let me know when you're on your way. Okay?"

"Okay. I could drive you over there and we could still practice during the drive. How's that sound?"

"Thanks, Scott. That would be great. Thank you so much."

"You're welcome. I'll call you in about an hour."

Eugenia ate the soup that Scott brought and then ran through a mock interview. She stood in front of him and practiced her "elevator" speech, a 30- second spiel that answers the question, tell me about yourself. He couldn't help but look at her gestures, her demeanor and just looked at her in wonderment. *She is absolutely what I need,* was his thoughts. Scott gave her tips on how to answer questions that they may ask. He asked her some of the questions that he has asked in an interview. He was so pleased that he could help her.

She changed into her navy blue pinned-striped suit with a skirt, stockings and pumps. She had put her hair in a bun, put on the smallest pair of earrings, a gold necklace, applied the right amount of makeup and topped it off with a subtle shade of lipstick. She grabbed her portfolio that contained several copies of her resume and a copy of the job application. As she came out of her bedroom, Scott stood up and his look stopped Eugenia in her tracks.

"I would kiss you but I know it would ruin your makeup. My God, you look stunning. But very professional, of course," he said with a nod.
Also, sexy, beautiful, and confident. My God, Eugenia, how did you come into my life?

"It's okay, right?" Eugenia said nervously, brushing a piece of lint off her skirt and blushing at the look that Scott was giving her.

"Yes, trust me." He then came over and kiss her lightly on the cheek. "I couldn't resist. You're going to knock 'em dead, babe…you ready?"

"Yes."

Eugenia sat with not only Pat, but two other library staff members. She was prepared with extra copies of her resume and offered each of them a copy. However, they gestured that they had them. Eugenia took deep breaths when answering the questions and she took notes during the time she was given to ask questions. Despite her nervousness, she felt confident and excited at the prospect of getting this job. And she was thankful that there was a familiar face present.

As she walked out of the library into the bright Maine sun, she could see Scott standing by his SUV, texting on his cell phone and waiting. He looked up as she approached him. She walked a little more slowly as she approached him. He was glad that she was walking slowly because he had to finish his text message. *This demeanor doesn't look good,* he thought. *We'll see.*

"Well, how'd it go?"

She stood there with a stoned look on her face, as if she was ready to cry. He remembered that same look that she gave him a few days ago, that "Chuck look" as what he called it, solemn, sober, and expressionless.

"Well, it wasn't what I expected. I think I better sit down."

He went to the passenger side, opened the door and Eugenia climbed in. Then he came around and climbed into the driver's seat. Eugenia continued not to speak and had the same look. She then looked at him seriously.

"Babe, you're scaring me. For goodness sake, what happened?"

She swallowed. "Well, thank you for the tips. Some of the questions you asked were the same ones they asked, so I was prepared." She then looked at him with tears in her eyes.

"Scott, they offered me the job, right then and there. They said that pending all the background checks and all, I've got it if I want it. We'll go over salary within the next few days and iron out a couple more details. And I said yes."

Scott sat there mesmerized, not knowing what to say. This was it, the answer to his prayer. He grabbed her and kissed her, messing up her lipstick but neither cared. He held her for what seemed like forever. He pulled back and kissed her on her forehead.

"Congratulations. Eugenia, tell me," as he pulled away, looking at her, "How do you feel?"

She looked at him and took a long sigh, "I feel good about this, a little scared, but good. Everything has happened so fast. I've only been here a week. I was laid off two weeks ago. It's mind boggling, to say the least. But I'm good. Yeah, this is good," she said, nodding reassuringly.

"Well, we'll have to celebrate. What's your pleasure?"

"Gosh, I don't know."

"I've got an idea. Do you trust me?"

"Sure, I trust you." She couldn't believe she said that, but it was true. She *did* trust him.

"Okay. Great. I'm going to take you home and I want you to dress warmly, although I know it's hot, but, trust me, you'll need to dress like that because of what we're going to do. Then we'll take it from there."

"Does this involve your motorcycle?"

"Ok, you guessed it. But after the ride, I have another surprise. Okay?"

"Sure."

Chapter 16

The Letter

They stopped by the cottage and Eugenia put on a pair of jeans, tennis shoes, a red University of Maryland Terrapins sweat shirt and took her hair out of the bun, combing it to the side with the other side tucked behind her ear. She washed her face and removed her makeup. She exited the bedroom and looked around for her purse. Scott had seated himself on the couch in front of the still cluttered coffee table that contained Eugenia's research. It dawned on her that she hadn't done much with it for several days. She knew she had to organize it and the paperwork sat, waiting for her attention. *I'll get to it*, she thought.

They drove over to Scott's and got ready for the motorcycle ride on his Honda Gold Wing. He helped her with the helmet, packed her purse in the convenient trunk on the back of the bike, put on his helmet and climbed onto the bike. He then tuned the radio to a local station that played old time rock and roll. Eugenia was surprised that this motorcycle had a radio. Very cool.

Okay, can this guy look any sexier sitting on this bike? she thought. *Geez! Yikes! I guess there's something about a guy wearing a black leather jacket, blue jeans, boots, straddling a motorcycle. Damn!*

Scott showed her how to get on the bike and she followed his directions. The seat was surprisingly comfortable and roomy. She situated herself and discovered that she had a choice of holding onto the convenient handles on the side or onto him, around his waist. *I'll just wrap my arms around his waist* and she placed her arms around him, taking in the now-familiar soapy smell of Scott combined with the smell of the leather jacket. *Okay, is this heaven or what?* thought Eugenia. *This is sexy.*

They sped off heading north on Rt. 1 and ending up at Camden Hills State Park. They followed a winding road that continued up a hill. Scott and Eugenia eventually parked the bike in a parking lot and walked a short distance to a view that was, to say the least, breathtaking. With other tourists, hikers, families around, they viewed Camden Harbor and Penobscot Bay and the view was no less spectacular! There was a variety of lush green trees, a harbor full of various sizes and makes of boats, the town of Camden with several church steeples towering over the smaller buildings, and, off into the distance, Penobscot Bay leading into the Atlantic Ocean. Scott and Eugenia just stood there and took in the view. Scott mentioned that in the fall a magazine rated Camden Bay and this view as one of the best places to view the fall foliage. Eugenia could understand why. They climbed the narrow spiral staircase of the nearby stone structure, ending up at the top with an even better view of this Maine treasure. *Wow!* thought Eugenia.

After taking pictures, they got back unto the bike and headed down the mountain back to Scott's house and his second surprise for Eugenia. When they arrived, Eugenia noticed a container on the porch that stores and maintains food, keeping any hot food hot.

"This is part of your surprise," Scott said as he opened the front door and lifted the container. "I had Julio, my head chef, throw together dinner. Just a little celebratory dinner."

"But you didn't know that I would get the job."

"No, I didn't. But you did get an interview and that's celebration enough."

They both went inside and Scott immediately headed into the kitchen.

"Make yourself at home. I'm just going to see if this needs anymore heat."

Eugenia took off her sweatshirt since it was a little too much for this warm Maine day. She had a t-shirt underneath. She removed her tennis shoes and socks. *Walking with bare feet in here just feels right. How did I get so comfortable in such a short period of time around him?* she thought. She started to settle down on the couch but then immediately got up and went into the kitchen to see if she could help out.

"Oh, no, this is for you. Just sit down there and I'll take care of this. Most of it is done anyway."

She sat at the kitchen table and watched Scott prepare the dinner. He occasionally looked over and smiled as he went about warming up the chowder, putting the lobster rolls and roasted potatoes in the oven and putting the salad in the refrigerator. Having poured a glass of wine for both of them, he occasionally took a sip while continuing his tasks. The windows were open and a welcoming Maine breeze came through the kitchen. Eugenia realized how much she enjoyed the lack of humidity and how the summers up here weren't like D.C.'s humidity-laden days that would zap you of energy by mid-afternoon. She didn't miss that a bit. She got up and, taking her glass of wine with her, went over to the back door stared out into his back yard through the screened door, remembering how the five of them sat a few days ago laughing and drinking out on the patio.

She stood outside looking at the various houses that surrounded Scott's, looking at the trees and rose bushes in the neighbors' yards and noticing the hydrangea bushes that seemed to be everywhere in this town. They bloomed delightfully in the August sun. This was truly a beautiful place. Eugenia realized that this was home. She had returned to the place of her ancestor; she was possibly walking on the same soil that he walked. She was able to see Ezekiel Benjamin Freeman's island. Now she was going to write his story so that he can be a part of local and Maine history. She knew she had it in her. After all, his blood was running through her veins.

Eugenia and Scott sat in the dining room at a table decorated with a white linen table cloth, fine china, and lit candles. They dined on the chowder that Julio had prepared. It reminded her of the first night that they had met.

When she entered the dining room a few minutes ago, she was in awe at what Scott had done. "Scott, this is so thoughtful. Thank you so much."

"You're more than welcome. So Aunt Nell and Sophia got back okay?"

"Yeah, Sophia sent me a text and they're safe and sound back home."

Scott told her how pleased he was at meeting them both and how Chuck had mentioned Aunt Nell quite often. He felt as if he knew her when they finally met. Eugenia then told Scott more about the interview and her anticipation about the new job. They talked about the commute to Rockland and how it compares to the nightmare commutes back in D.C.

"That I won't miss a bit," she stated, as she took a spoonful of chowder. Scott must have learned this in restaurant school in that he brought out each course separately. They ate, talked, laughed and drank the wine. Eugenia was so excited but she knew that there was quite a bit to do to settle into her new home.

Everything was so delicious and they finished eating. Eugenia helped Scott clean up the dining room and take everything back into the kitchen. Afterwards they settled into the living room and Eugenia took her now-familiar place on the couch, tucking one leg under the other. The Pandora station played in the background, a smooth jazz station, no doubt. Scott sat down beside her and Eugenia noticed that he seemed to get quiet all of a sudden, while she babbled on about her new job. He had a solemn look on his face and seemed to have wandered off somewhere. She looked at him and asked:

"Are you all right?"

He leaned forward, elbows resting on his knees, looking down at the floor. Moving his hands through his hair and with his elbows still on his knees, he looked over at Eugenia and at first didn't say anything.

"Okay, you're scaring me. What's going on, Scott?" She had untucked her leg and was leaning forward. Scott then got up, walked over to the stairs and headed up to his bedroom, not saying a word. He returned with an envelope. Sitting beside her, took his glasses that were propped on top of his head and put them on. Eugenia sat upright, staring at the envelope, not knowing what to think. *What's going on?* she thought.

"Eugenia, your Aunt Nell gave this to me." He then showed her the envelope and she immediately recognized the handwriting, her name spelled out in her father's handwriting. She covered her mouth, took a breath and froze.

"Your Aunt Nell gave it to me and wanted me to open it and read it to you. She didn't think you'd be able to read it yourself."

"Well, she's right about that. Why did she give it to you? When did she give it to you? Why didn't she give it to me? Why didn't she read it herself?" Eugenia said defensively.

"Trust me, I asked the same thing. Remember last night when we had all gone into the living room while you were still cleaning up in the kitchen."

Eugenia nodded.

"That's when she gave it to me. So, anyway she said that Chuck's instructions were that you were to get this after his death. Apparently, he wrote this maybe a year or so before he died. She said that he had been feeling bad, had some heart problems, high cholesterol and felt like he should write this to you while he was able to. His instructions to her were to wait about six months after he died, to give you time to grieve. He wanted you to receive the letter while you were here in Camden. He also told her to use her judgment as to who would be able to read it to you. She knew that she couldn't. So he said that either Sophia could read it or anyone else that Aunt Nell chose, maybe not family but a close friend. So she chose me."

"Again, why you?"

"Aunt Nell had heard a lot about me from Chuck. Apparently he had told her quite a bit. I didn't know that. But then when she came here...," he then took a breath and continued, "she could see that I had feelings for you. She thinks that Chuck wanted us to meet or wanted to introduce me to you, but that never happened. He mentioned to me several times how he couldn't get you up here. You were very busy with your career and all. So Aunt Nell realized my feelings for you. When she gave me this letter, I was just as surprised as you are. But she let me know that she saw something between us and that she knew she was making the right choice. I told her that I would be honored to take it and read it to you and that she was right about how I felt about you. Eugenia, I have fallen in love with you."

Eugenia sat looking at Scott with tears welling up in her eyes and in almost a whisper, she said:

"She made the right choice. She was always so good with reading people." Tears began to stream down her cheeks and Scott retrieved a box of tissues from the nearby bathroom. He wiped her tears and she grabbed a tissue to blow her nose. He pulled her in his arms and hugged her tightly before pulling away. Scott went into the dining room and retrieved the bottle of wine that sat on the dining room table, poured some for the both of them and sat back down on the couch. Picking up the letter from the coffee table, he looked at Eugenia and said:

"Well, are you ready for this?"

She then looked at him and nodded. As he fumbled with the envelope, she interrupted him.

"Wait." Eugenia interrupted. He stopped and looked at her.

"She picked the right person."

"Good, I was wondering. Like I said, I was surprised as you...I thought..."

She then interrupted, "Because, Scott, I love you, too. She could see that. I'm just so surprised at my feelings for you. This has happened so quickly. I met you a week ago and you are just what I need. I even like your corny jokes. I love the way you make me feel, I feel so comfortable with you, so at ease. I think about you all the time and want to be with you all the time. I feel we can talk about anything; I feel like I can tell you anything. I feel protected when I'm in your arms. I feel needed, wanted, loved. I don't ever remember feeling this way...ever. I love you, Scott Mackey!"

Scott then grabbed her and kissed her passionately and he held her tighter than before.
"Babe, you have made me so happy. I am overjoyed. I love you so much."

They embraced for a few minutes more. As they pulled away, Scott brushed Eugenia's hair back and placed kisses on her cheeks and her face. They looked into each others' eyes and he continued to kiss her, placing brief kisses on her lips. Then he turned his attention back to the letter.

"Are you ready for this?" he asked. He then told her to lay back and use the recliner on the couch. After she was comfortable and she turned on her side, facing him, he put his glasses back on, sat facing her, opened the envelope and began:

My Dearest Eugenia,

I gave this letter to your Aunt Nell and asked her three things—to give this to you after my death and to pick an appropriate time to give it to you—that was up to her. I also asked her to wait, and not give this to you too soon after my death—to hold off. It was of her choosing to give it to you or she could have someone else present it.

First, and foremost, I love you with all my heart. I have always been proud of everything you've done with your life. Even though there were times we disagreed, I've always been proud.

I wrote this letter because I know that my health is failing and I wanted to write this while I'm able to think straight. This letter is mainly about your mother. She was a treasure and the love of my life. I know we've had many conversations about her. But we haven't had a lot of talk about her family and her ties to Camden, Maine, other than that's why I bought the cottage there. I hope you've visited there and have discovered the scrap book in my closet and the many treasures that it holds. Hopefully Aunt Nell has told you about this. Your mother had a connection to that town and I was trying to research this. A lot of this research involves computers and you know how I am about those—not good. But I know you have a better grasp and can continue with the research.

Just then the Pandora radio station began playing an instrumental version of "Stairway to the Stars". Scott stopped reading abruptly and looked at Eugenia. They both smiled.

"Wow, that's weird. Do you hear what's playing? Oh, my God, how appropriate. Well let me continue reading. I think Chuck would have liked that." He continued, "Where was I? Oh yeah…"

It is my wish that you find those roots, discover what made her the priceless gem that she was and, in turn, learn something about yourself. Negro Island Lighthouse is somehow a part of you. This history should be a part of the history of that area. I only wish that I could have given that to you—but I know you can uncover this story. You have a gift and you should use it to tell this story. Take care, daughter.
Love, Daddy.

Scott stopped once more, still staring at the letter. "Oh, my God, Eugenia." She looked at the surprised look on his face, obviously there was something there that he hadn't read. He looked up at Eugenia with a face of sheer terror and surprise. "Listen to this..."

P.S. And if you ever get to Camden, please look up my friend, Scott—a true gentleman. He owns a restaurant called Fins that is on the water. We spent many hours drinking, shooting the breeze about D.C. and he plays a mean piano. Tell...,

Scott then paused, took a breath and continued, choking on his words.

Tell him hello. I think you'll like him.

Take care of yourself, sweetheart.

Scott held the letter in his hands and stared at it for a few minutes. He just couldn't believe what he just read. Eugenia moved beside him, removed the letter from his hand and placed it on the coffee table. She took his hand and squeezed it. Taking one of the tissues, he wiped his eyes after removing his glasses. She placed her arms around him, held him and rubbed his back. A myriad of emotions ran through both of them—everything from surprise to serenity to grief.

"Wow, I didn't expect that. This has been a few days of surprises—first Aunt Nell entrusted me with his letter and then Chuck thought highly enough of me to mention me in it. I am so humbled I can't even speak."

Turning to Eugenia, Scott said, "You know, it's a unique feeling when someone puts their trust in you. It's special." They both sat there in silence for a few minutes, Eugenia rubbing his back, Scott with his elbows resting on his knees.

"Well, it looks like you're well ahead of what your dad wants you to do with the research and all. As they say 'great minds think alike' "

"Yeah, isn't that something. We were always on the same wave length."

Scott turned to Eugenia and asked, "Are you okay? I mean this letter is such a surprise. Are you okay?"

"I'm fine. I thought I'd be upset, but I'm really okay. It's nice, it really is. It's kind of weird, but I thought when I entered the cottage and then his room, I thought I'd get really upset and couldn't stay there. But I felt safe, or some sort of relief. I was glad to be somewhere that he loved and cherished. I feel the same with this letter—some sort of degree of feeling safe and loved. It's hard to explain."

"No, I understand, because I'm feeling the same," he said as he kissed her on her forehead.

"Eugenia, I hope this doesn't sound strange, but I would like for you to stay with me tonight. We don't have to have sex, although that would be awesome. But I need you beside me. Even if you stayed here on the couch, I need you here with me tonight. Besides, after this letter, I don't know how I could make love to you, at least not yet."

Eugenia looked at Scott. They both had felt the desire, the chemistry between them and they both had thought about making love. Eugenia couldn't recall Scott mentioning until now. Was she ready? She thought for a few minutes and then said, "Could you drive me home so that I could get a change of clothing?"

"So I guess that's a yes?"

"Yes, you already have a toothbrush for me."

The warm Maine breeze moved the curtains in the bedroom and the only light was from the streetlamp outside of the window. Scott slept on his back in only his pajama bottoms. She snuggled up beside him, hung unto his arm and rested her head against his arm. She kissed his shoulder and whisper, "I love you, Scott," and dozed off, falling asleep quickly.

Scott felt her hair against his arm, opened his eyes briefly and uttered, "I love you too, babe," and then returned to his slumber.

Epilogue—Eugenia

Journal Entry
Sunday, August 30, 2015

The next two weeks were a whirlwind of activity. I had begun the process of selling my condo and was back and forth between Maryland and Maine, settling my affairs. Although I knew it would take more than two weeks, I had at least started the ball rolling. When my new employer, the Rockland Public Library— that sounds really cool to say — asked when I could start, I let them know two weeks, which is the typical time that one would take when giving notice about leaving a job. Besides, they were aware that I needed to relocate to Maine. I used this time to get things in order.

After returning to Maine and settling into my new job, I continued my research in order to get the story of Ezekiel Benjamin Freeman out and in print. With my connections now to the library and the area schools, the possibility of getting the finished product out and into the library and the schools was likely. I pressed on with the research and the subsequent book titled Negro Island Light: The Story of Ezekiel Benjamin Freeman. I intended to find out more about the five generations of women and their stories. Daddy wanted me to do that and I, more than ever, wanted to as well.

I found myself spending less and less time at the cottage and more and more time at Scott's house. I also was a regular fixture at Fins, sometimes helping in the kitchen, since I'm an expert chopper, but mostly sitting at the bar while Scott tickled the ivories of that beautiful piano. Even though it was nearing the end of the tourist season, the restaurant crowd seemed to grow. Apparently through word of mouth and social media, news of the piano man spread and people seemed to flock to Fins to hear him play. Amazing!

After that first night staying at Scott's, I found it hard to lie beside him and not make love. Scott made it clear that it was up to me, that he wanted me, but was patient. The first night that we made love, all five of my senses seemed to come alive. What's up with that? That's not the first time that has happened. It seems he brings out something in me that I didn't know existed. Or maybe, since I'm away from the rat race that I was a part of for so long, maybe I'm just noticing things I've never noticed before. Maybe it's a combination of both. Who knows!

First, I felt the warm Maine breeze come through the windows. It had a bit of coolness to it, indicating the impending change in the seasons, from summer to fall. I saw the light of the street lamp make its way into the room. That now familiar soapy smell that was Scott was prevalent. And the silence was only pierced by the sounds of our love making and the radio that played softly downstairs in the distance. He was attentive, placing gentle kisses from head to toe and I could feel the hairs from his full beard on my skin. When we held hands, I could see his slightly darker than ivory-colored skin against my light-caramel hue—Caucasian against black, European against African, two different cultures, together. His kisses were passionate and I could taste his sweet lips; his kisses were warm and gentle. His long piano fingers gently caressed my body. He constantly held me tight. He then sang in my ear the lyrics from "Truly" by Lionel Ritchie as it played on the radio. He caressed my cheek and looked into my eyes through the darkness, as he put the maroon comforter around my shoulders and he sang the romantic and poignant lyrics of a man professing his love to his woman.

We had found each other through a chance meeting. But I realize now that we would have eventually met—it was inevitable. I would have followed the instructions in Daddy's letter, found my way to Fins and said hello to Daddy's friend.

So this is my life now in a small town in Maine—working as a library historian, helping people uncover their past and their ancestors, studying history, writing history books about local African American history, loving a man who truly loves me, laughing at corny jokes, and singing. Yes, singing songs by Ella Fitzgerald and Etta James in a tight red dress that's not too short and accompanied by a really sexy bearded piano-playing man from D.C., who was a friend of Daddy's. Sophia was right—you never know what's around the corner, what's ahead of you. Sometimes you have a take a leap of faith. As corny and cliché as it sounds, often doors do open when other doors close.

I can honestly say I've never been happier.

The End

About the Author

Claudette Lewis Bard, a life-long Marylander, is a fan of romance and historical fiction novels. She got the writing bug in her first year of college while taking a remedial English 101 class. The teacher had her rewrite an assignment several times until she was able to translate her thoughts, to tell what was in her soul and put those feelings into words. She has written several short stories, a successful grant, an article for a community newspaper and a non-fiction narrative chronicling the lives of several elderly relatives. Negro Island Light is her first published novel. Claudette Lewis Bard lives in the Baltimore area with her husband, Ed, and two dogs, Jazz and Roxi.

CPSIA information can be obtained
at www.ICGtesting.com
Printed in the USA
BVOW06s0400290417
482700BV00004B/42/P

9 781367 280700